#1

Drat!
We're Rats!

Drat!
We're Rats!

Jahnna N. Malcolm

ISBN 0-0590-4191-6

A big bouquet of roses and warm thanks to the gang: Jesika Theos, Amma Rowan-Caneer, Faun Le Desma, Brittany Greenfield, Corena Howe, Juliana Wheeler, and Caitlin Maddigan

Cover photography by Christopher Briscoe

Printed in the United States

To Dash and Skye
The lights of our lives

Chapter One

"I hate ballet!"

Kathryn Margaret McGee crossed her arms and slumped down in the backseat of her family's blue station wagon. Mrs. McGee adjusted the rearview mirror to get a good look at her twelve-year-old daughter.

"Now, Kathryn – "

"Please don't call me Kathryn, Mom!" McGee interrupted. "You know I don't like that."

"All right...McGee." Her mother sighed and then continued. "Remember, we made a deal. If you went to ballet class one day a week, then you could play hockey and do whatever you liked on the other six days."

1

"But that was a class, Mom, in Stephanie Fritz's basement. This is different. This is doing silly ballet."

"It isn't silly," her mother declared as she flicked on the turn signal. "*The Nutcracker* is a beautiful ballet, and you should consider yourself very lucky if the Deerfield Academy of Dance allows you to be in their production."

"Lucky?" McGee tugged her stocking cap down over her chestnut-colored braids. She was missing practice with the Fairview Express, the hottest junior ice hockey team around. She didn't consider that lucky. Being the only girl on the team, McGee had fought hard to prove herself. She wasn't about to do anything that would endanger her position as a starter.

"Coach Briggs won't be too happy about me missing today's scrimmage."

"One practice won't matter," her mother announced. "He works you too hard as it is. Being in a ballet with other girls will be good for you."

"Good for me," McGee repeated to herself. "That's a laugh."

"What did you say, young lady?"

McGee glanced up and caught the warning look in her mother's eye. "Nothing," she mumbled.

Mrs. McGee nodded and turned her attention back to her driving. "Your two sisters just loved ballet. I can't understand why you don't feel the same way. It's so romantic. The music, the costumes – "

"The humiliation," McGee murmured under her breath. If the guys on her team knew she was auditioning for ballet, they'd laugh her off the ice.

"You know, Mom," McGee said, trying a different tactic, "if I get chosen to be in this ballet, I'll have to miss Stephanie Fritz's dance classes. She's very strict about that. She may even kick me out of class."

"Is that what you're worried about?"

McGee nodded solemnly.

"You don't have to worry about a thing. I already talked to Cathy, and she is very excited about this audition. If you're chosen, she's planning to bring the whole class to watch you dance."

"The whole class? Geez Louise!" McGee slumped back in her seat. Things were getting worse.

Her class consisted of ten very different girls ranging from nine to fourteen. They all lived on the edge of town in what was known as Fairview's farm community and took class together because their mothers had worked out a car pool system. McGee lived in an old white house surrounded by pasture land. She rode the bus to school and couldn't get anywhere without a car. Most of the families in Fairview were like hers – the parents worked in Deerfield or at Curtiss-Dobbs Air Force Base and wanted their kids to experience the "wonders of growing up in the country." McGee and her sisters felt they were only experiencing the hassles of it.

McGee leaned her head against the cool glass and stared out the window. She realized they had left the main road and were driving through Brooke Hollow, a familiar suburb of Deerfield.

"Hey, what're we doing?"

"We're picking up Mrs. Hays and her daughter, Gwendolyn."

"What?" McGee shouted, a little too loudly. "I thought we were going to the ballet audition."

"We are. You and Gwendolyn are auditioning together."

McGee groaned. Gwendolyn Hays was the same age as McGee, but that's where the similarities stopped. Because their mothers were close friends, the two girls were sometimes forced to socialize. That usually meant sitting through some dull "mother-daughter" tea, or a fashion show, or something equally boring.

"What's she doing in ballet, anyway? She's fat."

"Now, McGee, be nice!" her mother said. "Gwendolyn is *not* fat. She's just a little" – Mrs. McGee searched for the right word – "plump."

"Ha!" The last time McGee saw Gwendolyn Hays, she was fat. There were no two ways about it. Short red hair, thick glasses, stubby legs, pudgy arms – fat.

"She has been taking ballet lessons to trim down," Mrs. McGee said as they pulled into the driveway of a ranch-style brick home. "And I think it's really paid off."

"This, I've got to see."

From the look her mother gave her in the rearview mirror, McGee knew she had reached the danger point, so she decided to keep her mouth shut.

Gwendolyn Hays. Smart, talented Gwendolyn. She'd gotten straight A's ever since first grade and had been playing the piano from the time she was three. McGee's mother called Gwendolyn a "model child." McGee giggled to herself as she thought, a *fat* model.

Her mother put the car in park, lightly tapped the horn, then turned to face her daughter. "I know you don't want to do this, but just give it a chance, OK?"

McGee looked up at her mother and nodded. "OK."

"And be nice to Gwendolyn. I think she's really excited about this."

At that moment a short, round-faced girl with glasses stepped out of the front door, crossed her arms, and glared at them across the yard.

"If that's excitement, I'll eat my ballet shoes," McGee muttered.

Gwendolyn Hays didn't move a muscle until her mother, a tall, willowy blonde, grabbed her by the elbow and gently guided her down the sidewalk toward the car. She swung open the back door of the station wagon and tossed a pink patent leather bag with a picture of toe shoes painted on the front onto the floor. McGee could see that the dance bag was brand-new. The price tag still dangled from the zipper.

McGee waited for Gwen to say hello, but she said nothing. Instead, Gwen shut the door and sat staring straight ahead.

"Well, McGee," her mother prompted. "Say hello to Gwendolyn."

McGee turned and smiled stiffly. "Hi, Gwendolyn."

"It's Gwen." The girl squinted her eyes and hissed, "And I want you to know this is not my idea of a good time."

"I'm not exactly thrilled by it, either," McGee shot back.

"Didn't your mother call mine?"

"Well, if she did, I didn't have anything to do with it."

"Hmmph!" Gwen leaned against the window.

Same old Gwen, McGee thought to herself. *Unfriendly and unpleasant.*

McGee settled back in her seat and sighed. She could tell this mother-daughter outing was getting off to the same start as all the others.

Mrs. Hays opened the front door and, grinning broadly, slid beside Mrs. McGee.

"I'm so excited, Norma," Mrs. Hays chirped. "Our two girls together in ballet. I'm green with envy. I wish it were us."

"So do I!" Gwen grumbled. "Want to trade?"

Mrs. McGee laughed merrily and pulled out of the driveway.

While their mothers chattered away, the two girls rode the rest of the way in silence. McGee only half listened to them as she watched the drab scenery go by.

November in Ohio was always an in-between month. The pretty yellow and red leaves of autumn had disappeared but the usual winter carpet of white snow hadn't arrived yet. Everything looked brown and gray and a little dreary – just how she felt.

Soon they were in downtown Deerfield. They passed lots of people bundled up in winter coats, leaning into the wind as they walked along the sidewalks.

"Oh, look, girls," Mrs. Hays called. "There it is! Hillberry Hall."

McGee and Gwen sat forward and peered through the windshield. In front of them was a big granite building with at least a hundred steps leading to four large pillars. It looked like an old courthouse or county jail. The only indication that a ballet school might be hidden inside was the banner that stretched across the top pillars.

Gwen read the words out loud: "The Deerfield Academy of Dance presents *The Nutcracker* – December 17 and 18."

Mrs. McGee pulled the blue station wagon up to the curb and turned off the engine. "We're here."

McGee and Gwen swallowed hard as they watched groups of young girls with tote bags climb the stairs to the big glass doors.

Mrs. Hays turned in her seat. "Do you want us to go in with you?"

"NO!" Gwen and McGee shouted back in unison. They recognized the fear in each other's eyes. Fear that their mothers would go with them and do or say something *really* embarrassing that they'd never live down.

"We'll handle this," Gwen said, adjusting her glasses. "I'm sure it's very simple. We just go up there, do a couple of steps around the room, and then get right out."

"So why don't you go shopping or something," McGee added, "and we'll meet you afterward."

McGee grabbed her ballet shoes with a rubber band holding them together and quickly hopped out of the car. Gwen did the same, nearly falling onto the sidewalk. Then, to the girls' horror, both mothers got out of the car.

"Oh, Gwennie," Mrs. Hays called. "Don't forget your dance bag." She handed Gwen the pink tote.

"Thanks." Gwen snatched at the strap and the bag hit the ground with a *thunk.*

Mrs. McGee grabbed her daughter and hugged her tight. McGee peered sideways, hoping no one was witnessing this embarrassing display.

"Now I'm sure you'll both be wonderful." Mrs. McGee retied the ribbon on one of McGee's braids and patted her on the head.

"We'll be right here waiting for you." Mrs. Hays gave Gwen a final squeeze. "Aren't you both excited?"

Gwen and McGee looked at each other and answered in a monotone. "We're thrilled."

Then they turned and slowly trudged up the one hundred and two steps to their doom.

Chapter Two

"Oh, no!" Gwen groaned. "This is worse than I thought!"

The reception area of the Deerfield Academy of Dance was jammed with girls and their mothers, all talking at once. It was so loud Gwen had to cover her ears.

"Everybody, please listen!" A voice strained to be heard above the others.

McGee stood on her tiptoes to see who it was. She watched a white-haired lady, dressed all in purple, wave a clipboard in the air.

"This is the sign-up sheet," the woman trilled in her Russian accent. "Please, put a lee-tle check next to your name!"

All the mothers instantly rushed forward.

"What is this?" Gwen protested as one very determined mother brushed past her. "A stampede?"

"You lee-tle ballerinas may all change your clothes in the dressing room."

Gwen and McGee watched a few of the girls move timidly toward the curtained off area at the far end of the room.

"Remember," the strange lady called, "black leotards and pink tights."

"Tights!" Gwen's face went completely white. "Why do we have to wear tights?"

"Because people always wear them in ballet classes."

"Well, I can't!' Gwen shouted. The idea of squeezing her plump body into a stretchy suit was pure agony.

McGee put her hands on her hips and looked at Gwen suspiciously. "I thought you took lessons."

"I do." Gwen hissed. "But at my dance school we can wear anything we like, just so long as it's comfortable. I always wear this."

She was wearing a gray jogging suit. It had a pink stripe down each leg and looked very comfortable.

"Then what do you carry in that?" McGee pointed to the pink bag that Gwen had nearly forgotten in the car.

"A leotard and tights," Gwen admitted. "But that's only to make my mother feel better. She studied

11

ballet when she was my age and got to dance solo parts. She was really pretty good."

"I bet she was," McGee said, recalling how tall and willowy Gwen's mother was. "Your mom's really beautiful."

Gwen stared McGee straight in the face. "And I'm not."

"I didn't say that," McGee sputtered.

"No, but you were thinking it. You've always thought that." Gwen pushed her glasses up on her nose. What did McGee know about not being beautiful? She was perfect. Pretty, long brown hair, a turned-up nose with just a dash of freckles, and big green eyes. Perfect. Gwen's mother was always saying, "Darling, why can't you try to be more like Kathryn McGee? She's so well-rounded." Gwen grimaced. "I got the round part right," she thought aloud.

"What did you say?" McGee peered into Gwen's face.

With a start, Gwen realized she'd been muttering to herself.

"You were saying something about well-rounded," McGee said.

"Oh, yes!" Gwen laughed a little too loudly to make up for the embarrassment of being caught talking to herself. "My mother encourages me to be well-rounded. She's certain that any minute now

I'm going to be a dancer and the most popular girl in school, just like she was."

McGee had never heard Gwen chatter so much. Usually she just made sarcastic cracks under her breath. McGee also realized that she had never really been herself with Gwen. Their mothers always hovered over them, forcing them to get along.

"Mom tries to make sure I'm totally in fashion." Gwen continued. "She read in *Dance Magazine* that all the real ballerinas were carrying these bags, so she ordered one for me." Gwen patted the pink tote bag and grinned. "Mostly I use it to carry snacks."

Gwen unsnapped one of the pockets of the bag and showed McGee the contents inside – a sandwich, a diet soda, and a package of Twinkies.

Just then a few girls came out of the dressing room and stood beside their mothers. Each one had her hair pulled back in a perfectly smooth bun and was dressed in regulation black and pink.

"I hate to break it to you," McGee whispered, "but this audition looks serious."

They both watched in silence as the dancers sat on the floor of the reception area, warming up. Their legs were stretched out in perfect splits. With their arms held in beautiful ovals above their heads, they gracefully touched their chests to the floor.

"Ouch!" McGee muttered. She was pretty limber but not that limber.

Gwen suddenly got a clear picture of herself being made a fool of in front of all those ballerinas. "I've got to get out of here."

McGee grabbed her arm. "You can't leave."

"Why not?" Gwen asked.

"Because!"

"Because?" Gwen shot McGee a withering look. "That's no reason."

"Because your mom will be mad, and well..." McGee swallowed hard and whispered, "I don't want to be left alone. It looks scary."

Gwen was surprised and pleased to hear McGee admit that. She always seemed so cool. Gwen whispered back, "Then come with me."

McGee's green eyes widened as Gwen explained in a hushed voice, "We can tell our moms that hundreds of kids showed up."

"And they didn't need us!"

"Right!"

The two girls backed slowly toward the door.

"Girls! Yoo-hoo, girls!"

Gwen and McGee froze. The little old lady was waving a purple chiffon scarf at them.

"Are you talking to us?" Gwen tried to sound casual as the whole room turned to stare at her.

McGee felt her ears start to burn. They always did that when she was embarrassed.

"Why are you standing there," the woman sang out, "like, how you say – lumps?"

14

Gwen didn't like the word lump; it was too close to plump. "We were just going to – how you say? SCRAM!"

She dragged McGee into the hall.

"Let's run for it!"

They clattered down the stairs to the next floor. The sound of rapid footsteps clicked behind them. McGee grabbed the first door at the bottom of the stairs and tugged it open.

"In here! Quick!"

Gwen hopped inside and McGee shut the door behind them. The room was pitch-black and smelled like an old mop. They pressed their ears against the door until the footsteps went past and faded down the hall.

"Boy, that was close!" Gwen puffed, trying to catch her breath.

"Yeah!" McGee whispered. "But what do we do now?"

"Well," a new voice answered from the darkness, "you could start by getting off my foot!"

"Yikes!" Gwen and McGee screamed and lurched blindly into each other. Gwen tripped over a metal bucket and it hit the floor with a crash. Then a broom clunked her on the head and she shrieked and grabbed for what felt like a sink.

It seemed to take hours before all of the cleaning supplies stopped clanking.

"That was *very* cool," the voice remarked. "If that

lady didn't know we were in here before, she does now."

"Which lady?" McGee asked, peering hard into the darkness.

"The one with the Russian accent and the scarves."

"Are you hiding from her, too?"

"You think I hang out in closets for the fun of it?" the voice answered.

"We really don't care what you do," Gwen snapped. She was still smarting from being hit by the mop.

Gwen and McGee heard a tennis shoe squeak on the floor and then the voice mutter, "I've got to find a new spot. You jerks gave this one away."

The door opened, sending a shaft of light into the closet. The stranger, a slim girl in a shiny red jacket, stared out into the hall. Her black, curly hair hung to her shoulders and went every which way.

"Rocky." Gwen read the printing on the back of her jacket out loud.

"Yeah, what?" The girl spun to face them, her dark eyes flashing.

"I was just reading your jacket. It says, Rocky."

"That's my name." The girl put her hands on her hips. "Don't wear it out."

Before they could reply, she turned and marched down the hall.

"Rocky?" McGee repeated. "Who'd name their daughter Rocky?"

"Someone who knew her personality," Gwen answered.

After a minute, they stepped out of the closet and tiptoed toward the exit sign at the end of the hall.

"Oh, there you are!" a voice echoed behind them. "I have been look-ink everywhere for you."

Gwen moaned, "Oh, no."

From past experience she knew what would happen to her now. First, the Russian woman would tell her mother she'd tried to escape. Then her mother would have to apologize and *then* she'd have to take private lessons or sign up for something even more awful – like modeling or charm school. At least "well-rounded" McGee was going to get it, too.

"Hey! Wake up!" McGee was tugging on her arm. "It looks like she got Rocky." Gwen spotted the red jacket just behind the woman and laughed out loud.

"I am Miss Delacorte," the white-haired woman explained as she herded the three of them back up the marble stairs with little fluttery gestures. "The Academy receptionist. My lee-tle ballerinas are always getting lost in this huge drafty building. It is part of my job to keep track of you."

Before they knew it, Rocky, Gwen, and McGee were back in the office of the Deerfield Academy. This time it was almost deserted.

"Now, let's see." Miss Delacorte examined a checklist and pointed at Rocky. "You must be Rochelle Garcia, yes?"

Rocky gave a quick nod and then shot Gwen and McGee a look that said, "Just try to laugh."

Then Miss Delacorte put a long delicate finger to her lips and stared at Gwen. "I guess that you might be Gwendolyn Hays."

Gwen winced and pushed her glasses up on her nose. She hated being called Gwendolyn.

"And last, but not least" – Miss Delacorte lightly touched McGee on the shoulder – "Kathryn McGee."

A burst of piano music came from the rehearsal studio.

"Oh, my goodness!" Miss Delacorte gasped. "The auditions are about to begin." She pushed them toward the big, black curtains marked Dressing Room. "Hurry and change your clothes!"

Inside, wooden benches piled high with coats lined the walls. McGee and Rocky plunked their bags down on a makeup table and quickly changed into their dance clothes.

Gwen found a tall standing mirror and slipped behind it. She took a deep breath and reached into her pink tote bag.

There was no escaping it. She would have to wear the hideous pink tights and black leotard with capped sleeves. Gwen squeezed into them as quickly as she could. The leotard was tight in the sleeves and lumpy around the middle. It took all of her courage to step out from behind the mirror, but she managed it.

Gwen took one look at McGee and Rocky and felt a wave of relief wash over her. In their outfits, they looked almost as bad as she did.

McGee was wearing an old leotard that had been worn by both of her sisters. It had turned green from too many washings and her faded pink tights had a huge gaping hole in the right knee. Rocky tried to pull her wild hair into one big ponytail, but it already looked messy. She was still wearing her red satin jacket.

"Let's get this thing over with," Rocky grumbled.

"Right!" McGee hitched up her tights and then flipped one of her braids over her shoulder.

Gwen straightened her glasses and tried to suck in her stomach. Then all three of them marched defiantly into the audition.

Chapter Three

Rocky swung open the door to the ballet studio and thirty girls turned to gape at her. She would have backed out of the room if McGee and Gwen had not been standing behind her, blocking her escape.

The room was huge. It was at least four times the size of the ballet studio where Rocky normally took class. Of course, that studio was an all-purpose room at Curtiss-Dobbs Air Force Base, where her father was stationed. Dance class was just one of the activities held in the recreation building.

"Either you come in and join us, or leave and shut the door behind you." A tall, thin man with thick, graying hair stood in front of the wall of mirrors. He was dressed in gray slacks and a white pullover. Raising an eyebrow, he added, "Make up your minds."

Rocky felt a hand push against her back and she nearly fell into the room.

"Don't shove!" she hissed at McGee.

"She pushed me!" McGee protested, pointing an accusing finger at Gwen.

"Well, neither one of you was moving," Gwen snapped back.

"Silence!" the gray-haired man commanded. "And take your places at the back of the line."

All three girls shut up instantly and scrambled to the ballet *barre*. They stood behind a tall, thin black girl. Her back was turned to the teacher and she was totally absorbed in the paperback novel she held balanced on the *barre*.

"That's better," the man said and turned away to talk to the accompanist.

"Who does he think he is, anyway?" Rocky grumbled under her breath.

"Anton Largo," the girl next to them whispered over her shoulder. She even looked up from her book.

"So?" Rocky wasn't impressed.

"He's the head of the academy," the girl explained in a soft voice. "He used to be fabulously famous."

"Oh." Rocky took a good, long look at the man. Now she noticed the ballet slippers on his feet. And his gray slacks were really stretch dance pants.

"What do I care who he is?" Rocky shrugged defiantly. "Let him throw me out. It wasn't my idea to come to this stupid audition anyway."

Rocky thought about the previous Monday when her mother had caught her in a fist fight with the boy who lives next door. He had started it, but Rocky was winning when her mother broke it up.

"It's just not right for you to go around hitting people all the time," Mrs. Garcia had scolded. "You'd think you were trying to be rowdier than your brothers."

Her four older brothers certainly taught Rocky everything she knew about defending herself. From the time she was two they had picked on her. And she quickly learned not to complain about it to their father the sergeant. He didn't care whose fault it was – *everyone* got punished. Sergeant Garcia would either "confine you to quarters" which meant being sent to your room, or assign you to "KP," which was Air Force talk for Kitchen Police. That meant washing dishes for a week.

Sergeant Garcia ran their house like his own miniature air force. He always barked orders at them like, "March to your room," or, "Square yourself in front of your plate," or, "At ease." Instead of saying, "Dinner's at six o'clock," Sergeant Garcia would say, "The next meal will be at eighteen hundred hours."

Her father was tough and her brothers were

tough. No wonder Rocky was the toughest girl in the sixth grade.

She leaned forward and nudged the tall girl in front of her. "My mom said either I come here, or be grounded for a month."

"What'd Rocky say?" Gwen whispered from behind McGee.

Rocky started to repeat her words, but suddenly the pianist hit a loud chord that echoed around the drafty room and signaled the start of the audition.

"Thank you, Mrs. Bruce." Mr. Anton acknowledged, with a slight nod, the ancient woman behind the keyboard. She smiled back pleasantly and sat with her hands in her lap, waiting for him to give her the next signal to play.

"Now, everyone, please sit down where you are, and Miss Jo will tell you the story of *The Nutcracker.*"

"I can't wait," Gwen muttered.

The line of girls circled the room completely. Everyone dropped to the floor and sat cross-legged, waiting to see what would happen next.

The door to the studio opened and in swept a woman, dressed in a black leotard with a long black skirt, pink tights, and sandals. Rocky sucked in her breath without thinking. She had never seen anyone who looked so elegant.

"Who's that?" she whispered to the black girl, who motioned for Rocky to be quiet.

The woman's hair was jet-black, with dramatic streaks of silver running through it. She wore it back in a braided bun, coiled at the base of her neck. Her face, with its high cheekbones and firm chin, looked chiseled out of marble. Everything about her was long – her sweeping arch of a nose, her slender legs and arms. Even the woman's fingers seemed to stretch out forever before tapering to a delicate point.

"Good morning, everyone!" Her voice tinkled like a tiny bell. "I am Josephine York, but you may call me Miss Jo." She smiled and nodded her head in a graceful bow.

There was a shy murmur of greeting from the girls around the room. Rocky was surprised to hear her own voice join the others.

"Now each of you must tell me and the rest of the girls who you are. We'll go around the room, starting here." She pointed to a dark-haired girl seated by Mrs. Bruce at the piano.

"Good morning, Miss Jo." The girl stood up and made a sweeping curtsey. "I am Courtney Clay," she announced with a smug smile. "I have studied ballet here at the Academy for six years."

"What does she want? A medal?" Rocky cracked. Gwen snorted and McGee put her hand over her mouth to cover her giggle.

One by one, the girls called out their names. Finally the circle of introductions reached the girl in front of Rocky, who said softly, "My name is Suzannah Reed, but I prefer to be called Zan."

"Hello, Zan," Miss Jo said. "It's good to have you back with us at the Academy."

The girl flashed a brilliant smile, then dipped her head shyly. It was Rocky's turn next. She gritted her teeth, stood up and announced gruffly, "Rochelle Garcia. But anybody who knows me calls me Rocky."

Over by the piano, the girl named Courtney Clay and a couple of friends laughed out loud. Rocky felt her cheeks turn red and she narrowed her eyes in their direction. Then she dropped back to the ground with a thud.

After witnessing Rocky's embarrassment, McGee decided it would be simpler not to explain her nickname. She popped up and blurted, "I'm McGee." Then she sat down quickly, hoping Gwen would jump in fast. It didn't work.

"But what's your last name?" Miss Jo asked.

"McGee."

Miss Jo paused for a moment, a confused look on her face. "McGee McGee?"

This caused another loud explosion of giggles from the girls over by the piano. McGee vigorously shook her head, her braids flopping around her shoulders. "No. My whole name is Kathryn McGee but I like to be called McGee."

"Oh, I see." Miss Jo nodded. "Like people call Rochelle Rocky."

"Right." McGee sunk back down on the floor, totally humiliated. Farther up the line, she heard someone whisper, "McGee McGee!" and then snicker.

Gwen decided she would stay put on the floor. She felt pudgy and ugly in her leotard. No way was she going to let herself be laughed at by the whole room. She leaned forward with her arms folded across her midriff to hide her stomach, and announced, "I am Gwen Hays."

"Do you have a problem, Gwen?" Miss Jo asked. "Stand up. Are you ill?"

"No, no, of course not!" Gwen snapped, wishing the floor would open up and swallow her. So much for her smart idea. In trying to hide her body she had called attention to it. *I'm never moving from this position as long as I live,* she vowed silently.

Luckily Miss Jo brought the focus back to herself. "Every year the Ballet of Deerfield performs *The Nutcracker* for the Christmas Season, and every year young dancers like yourselves audition for it. It is a grand tradition that has been going on since – " She laughed lightly. "Since before my hair was gray. In fact, some of the Academy's leading ballerinas were once in the very same position as you."

Rocky watched as some of the girls sitting toward the front squeezed each other in excitement, imagining themselves as grown-up ballerinas.

"Many of them had never even seen *The Nutcracker* before. Some of them didn't even know the story."

The girls who knew the story and had seen the ballet laughed a little too loudly in amazement. The rest, which included Rocky, Gwen, and McGee, sat in sheepish silence.

"Now, who can tell me what the ballet is about?"

Miss Jo looked around the room and nobody moved. Finally she said, "Zan, I'm sure you know the story."

The girl sitting next to Rocky looked up, startled. "Yes, I do." Her voiced cracked, and she quickly looked back down at the book she had cradled in her lap.

"Well, can you tell us what you know?"

Zan nodded miserably and then took a deep breath. At first her voice was so soft, the girls could hardly hear her. "It's about a little girl named Clara who is given a magical nutcracker for Christmas. That night, she falls asleep and dreams that the nutcracker is an incredibly handsome soldier. In the ballet he's called a Cavalier."

As Zan wove the romantic tale, her eyes sparkled and her voice grew stronger. "Clara has to help her

Cavalier do battle against the wickedly evil Mouse King. She throws her satin slipper at the King and they win the battle. Then..." Her voice became soft and dreamy. "Then the handsome Cavalier takes her in his beautiful sleigh to the magical Kingdom of Sweets. All sorts of groups dance for Clara, including the Sugar Plum Fairy, who is my personal favorite. She's so exquisite – "

"Exquisite?" one of the girls by the piano repeated snidely.

Zan stopped in mid-sentence, realizing she'd gotten carried away. She felt as if she'd been splashed with water and her voice fell to a dull whisper. "Some more people dance, the Cavalier takes Clara back home, and then she wakes up."

When Zan finished she immediately looked back down at the book she was reading.

Miss Jo's eyes widened in surprise and she said, "Well, yes, I guess that is the basic story. Thank you, dear." She smiled at Zan, who didn't look up. Miss Jo turned to the rest of the group.

"Zan got the beginning right but she left out just a few details in the second act. Can anyone remember any of the dances in the Kingdom of Sweets?"

One red-haired girl called out, "The Waltz of the Flowers." As the discussion continued, Gwen and McGee carried on their own conversation in the back of the class.

"I think I'll go for the part of Clara," Gwen whispered. "If all she does is lie in bed and dream, I would be perfect."

Zan looked up from her book just long enough to say, "Clara dances with the Cavalier. She's much older and has to be a perfectly wonderful dancer."

"Oh, well," Gwen sighed. "Forget that."

"Look on the bright side," McGee said, "Maybe they won't need us."

"Oh, I wouldn't count on it," Zan whispered. "They need party guests, mice, flowers, and dolls. That should just about use everyone here."

"Hey," Rocky chimed in, "maybe we'll get to wear pretty costumes." Sometimes Rocky's mother let her try on her beautiful formal gowns and she loved it – waltzing around the room in silk and satin. Of course she would die if her brothers ever found out.

"The costumes are absolutely gorgeous," Zan added, "but no matter what you wear, it still means getting up in front of thousands of staring eyes and embarrassing yourself."

"Thousands?" Gwen and McGee nearly choked on the word.

"That's right," Zan blinked her big brown eyes at them. "The performances are at Patterson Auditorium, the big brick building by the park. That seats exactly two thousand six hundred and seventy people, not to mention standing room."

Rocky eyed her suspiciously. "What makes you so smart?"

"It's on the bulletin board out front." Zan shrugged. "Anyone could read it."

"Oh." Rocky crossed her arms and stared at Zan. "I don't like your attitude."

"Don't worry," Zan replied pleasantly. "You won't have to put up with it for very long. You see, I won't be appearing in this ballet."

"How do you know that?" McGee asked.

Zan very carefully placed a bookmark in the mystery she was reading, set the book on the floor beside her, and announced in a low tone, "I know, because exactly five minutes after this audition starts...I am going to fall down and sprain my ankle."

Chapter Four

"The combination is simple," Miss Jo said, stepping in front of the class to demonstrate. "First the *adagio*, or slow part. I would like each of you to walk beautifully for four counts." Miss Jo circled gracefully around the room with her arms out and head held high.

She looks like a queen, Zan thought as Miss Jo passed by. Zan had really liked having Miss Jo as a teacher the past summer. It was the girls in her class she couldn't bear. They had teased Zan unmercifully about her height.

Of course, everyone did that. It wasn't easy being the tallest person in the sixth grade. It was even

31

harder being the tallest girl in all of Stewart Elementary School. The fact that she was so skinny didn't help. Most of the time she kept her head buried in a book and ignored their teasing.

"Now, after the *adagio*, I would like to see two *arabesques*." Miss Jo stood on one leg, her other leg extended out behind her. "Then for the finish – run, run, *grande jeté*." This time Miss Jo gestured for Courtney Clay to show the class.

Zan felt her body tense. Courtney, whose mother was on the Academy's board of directors, was the best dancer in the sixth grade. She was also the girl who had been the meanest to Zan the previous summer.

Courtney took her position, did the *adagio*, then ran and leaped in the air, her legs in a perfect split. She landed without a sound and a round of applause broke out from her little circle of friends.

"Big deal," Rocky grumbled.

"I can't do that." Gwen turned to McGee, panicked. "She can't expect me to. My legs just don't go that way."

"You'll be fine," McGee whispered. "It's just a leap. Pretend you're jumping over a mud puddle."

"I never jump over puddles. I always walk around them." Gwen slumped against the ballet *barre*.

"Some of the parts are more difficult than others," Miss Jo said. "So first I would like to see you dance. Then we will divide up into groups according to skill."

"Skill?" Gwen grumbled. "Nobody said we had to have skill."

Miss Jo picked up a tambourine. "Line up in the corner and we'll go one at a time."

"One at a time!" Zan's heart instantly sped up. The thought of everyone staring at her while she tried to dance was terrifying. With her long bony legs and arms, she felt like a huge, clumsy giraffe.

No matter how hard Zan tried to avoid getting up in front of people, she was always being forced into it. In September she had been chosen to represent her class in the school spelling bee. She stood on the stage in front of the entire school, towering over the rest of the contestants, and was so embarrassed that she missed her very first word.

The year before, she was picked to carry the flag for All-American Day. Her hands shook so much that the flag quivered during the whole ceremony.

But the worst thing had happened on Friday in gym class. Friday was square dancing day. She and Buddy Kelly, the most handsome boy in Stewart Elementary, were picked to demonstrate the new steps. When they stepped in front of the class he raised up on tiptoe and asked, "How's the weather up there?" The whole class laughed and she just stared at the floor like a goon. Then the music started and she skipped the wrong way, stepping on Buddy Kelly's foot. He hopped around acting like she'd broken it. This made the class laugh even harder.

Zan vowed right then and there that books were much better than people. They would never hurt you, and when you read them you could be any person and any height you wanted to be.

Suddenly, Mrs. Bruce struck the first few notes on the piano. She hit them so hard her large arms flapped against her side.

The pounding music matched the rhythm of Zan's heart. She took a couple of deep breaths and tried to calm herself. Her mystery novel was still clutched tight in her hand, and she quickly flipped it open to page 133. That was where Tiffany Truenote, teen detective, faked a sprained ankle so she could leave the ballroom and catch the thief who stole the debutante's jewels.

"If it worked for Tiffany, it can work for me," she told herself. None of this would be necessary if her parents hadn't forced her to attend the audition.

"You spend all day with your nose in some mystery novel." Her mother had said. "It's not at all healthy. You need fresh air, exercise, and friends."

Zan still couldn't figure out how being cooped up in a stuffy ballet studio with a bunch of snobby girls was going to give her fresh air and friends, but she went along with her parents – mostly because they had threatened to take away her library card if she didn't.

Zan practiced looping one foot behind her ankle. Out of the corner of her eye she could see Rocky, McGee and Gwen staring at her. Ever since she had let them in on her plan, they had been eyeing her closely.

"Walk, walk, *arabesque*," Miss Jo sang out as she beat the tambourine in time with the music. "And run, run, LEAP!"

Zan watched as one by one the girls with the perfect bodies fluttered gracefully across the room. She recognized a few of them, like Page Tuttle, a pretty blonde and Courtney's best friend. She also remembered Alice Wescott, a thin, mousy girl with light brown hair. Alice was a fourth-grader and the youngest in Courtney's circle of friends.

Then another blond girl with extra curly hair took her starting position and flashed a big friendly smile at the room.

"First the adagio," Miss Jo sang out.

The girl held her arms straight out to the side and walked like a person on a tightrope, nearly losing her balance with every move.

"*Arabesque!*"

Mrs. Bruce hit a chord on the piano just as Miss Jo banged the tambourine. It frightened the curly haired girl so much that she yelped and tripped over her feet.

Zan gasped as the girl fell with outstretched arms and skidded across the room on her stomach.

The music stopped and Miss Jo raced to kneel by the stunned girl.

"I'm OK, honest!" the blonde said in a giggly southern accent. "This kind of thing happens to me all the time."

Miss Jo's brow was knit with concern. "What's your name again?"

"Mary Bubnik." She grinned sheepishly. "My mother bought me some new shoes yesterday, and I think they may be a little too big."

"Well, Mary Bubnik," Miss Jo said as she helped the girl to her feet. "Do you want to try it again, from the beginning?"

"OK," Mary giggled. "But the same thing will probably happen again."

"Oh, great," Gwen groaned. "She's going to be put with our group."

"Speak for yourself," Rocky whispered. "I plan to be dancing with that group over there." She pointed to the girls gathered around Courtney Clay.

"This I gotta see," Gwen cracked.

Rocky stuck out her tongue at Gwen, then turned to smirk at Zan. "Well, one thing's for certain, you can't sprain your ankle now."

"Why not?" Zan asked.

"Because it will look phony."

"She's right," Gwen chimed in. "I mean, how would it look, two people in a row?"

"It'd look like you were a real klutz," McGee said, tugging at her tights. The hole in the knee immediately expanded and another run shot up her leg. "Darn!"

"Look who's a klutz?" Rocky chuckled at McGee.

"Who are you calling a klutz?" McGee challenged.

"You!" Rocky yanked one of McGee's braids. "You certainly couldn't be called a ballerina."

If there was one thing McGee hated, it was having her hair pulled. Before she knew what she was doing she punched Rocky in the shoulder.

"Go on, McGee, let her have it," Gwen urged. "She deserves it."

Rocky spun to face Gwen and her elbow jammed into Zan's stomach accidentally.

"Ooof!" Zan doubled over.

"You better watch it, Chubs," Rocky hissed directly into Gwen's face.

"CHUBS!" Gwen shrieked.

"Silence!" Miss Jo ordered. "I will not have this!"

The girls all froze where they were – Zan clutching her stomach; Gwen and Rocky nose to nose; and McGee with her fist raised, ready to punch Rocky again.

"If you want to join a boxing club, do so. This is a ballet studio. If you wish to remain here you must behave yourselves."

Miss Jo's voice was low and strong. She didn't need to shout. Her message came across loud and clear.

The girls mumbled apologies and shuffled as far away from each other as possible.

After a moment, Miss Jo said quietly, "That's better. The four of you will join Mary Bubnik and go next, please."

Gwen opened her mouth to protest but thought better of it. Miss Jo wasn't in any mood for an argument.

They all moved to join the blonde on the other side of the room. Zan kept her eyes glued to the ground. As she took her starting position, several girls started to giggle. The sound made her look up.

Reflected in the mirror was the oddest group of misfits she'd ever seen.

The blonde girl looked like a puppy dog, smiling and giggling every which way. The pudgy girl named Gwen was having trouble forcing her thick legs into a starting position. McGee, in braids, crouched over as if she were ready to sprint in the fifty-yard dash. Rocky, with her red satin jacket and wild hair, stood with her hands on her hips, glaring at everyone. And head and shoulders above them all stood Zan, a thin black girl with a terrible slump.

In one awful moment Zan saw the future. She would be cast in the ballet. She would make a fool of herself in front of thousands of people. Worst of all, she would be dancing with a bunch of losers.

Miss Jo clapped her hands. "Let the audition begin."

Chapter Five

"Boy, oh, boy," Mary Bubnik announced in her southern twang, "I don't know about y'all, but I sure am glad that's over."

The auditions were done. Miss Jo had left the room with Mr. Anton to make up the cast list. Now the girls had to wait for the results.

Mary Bubnik looked around the room for a friendly face. Over by the piano, a group gathered around the pretty brunette named Courtney, hanging on her every word. They didn't look like they wanted company.

Another group was leaning against the ballet *barre* on the far wall, whispering in hushed tones. They looked awfully tense.

Finally Mary Bubnik turned to the girl with the wild hair standing beside her. "What part do you think we'll get?"

"*We?*" Rocky repeated.

Mary nodded. "I hope it's the dancing flowers. My mother and I saw the ballet last year in Oklahoma. All the girls from my tap and baton twirling class went with their mothers. We all agreed that the flowers had the nicest costumes by far. They have these pretty pink tutus that look like little fluffs of clouds when you jump."

Rocky stared at Mary Bubnik in amazement. "I don't know about you, but I *know* they're not going to give me a part after what just happened."

"Me, neither," McGee chimed in.

Zan slumped against the wall and nodded in agreement.

"Oh, that's right," Mary said, suddenly remembering their little skirmish. "Gee, well, I'm sorry for y'all."

"What's everybody so depressed about?" Gwen shoved her glasses up on her nose. "Isn't this what we wanted?"

"Hey, you're right," Rocky agreed. "We should be celebrating." She clapped Gwen on the back and gave her a friendly smile.

Gwen still resented Rocky calling her "Chubs" but it was always nice to receive a compliment. She decided to write off the insult to "the heat of the moment," and smiled back.

"I have to be in *The Nutcracker*," Mary Bubnik groaned. "I just have to!"

All four of them turned to stare at her. "You *want* to be in this?" McGee asked.

"Oh, yes," Mary Bubnik said. "Ever since my mother saw the audition notice, that's all she's talked about."

Mary didn't mention why it was so important to her mother. Mary's parents had divorced the summer before, and ever since her life had been turned upside down. She and her mother moved to a tiny apartment in Glenwood, a suburb of Deerfield, while her brother stayed in Oklahoma with Mary's father. For the first time in her life, Mary didn't have any friends.

Mrs. Bubnik was always coming up with "fun girl things" for them to do. She'd come home from work and say, "Let's go out for a pizza. Wouldn't that be fun?" Or, "It'd be fun to have our hair done." The one she said most often was, "Isn't this fun? Two bachelorettes on our own!"

Mrs. Bubnik spent three months trying to help Mary make friends. She had enrolled her in everything, but so far it had been a complete disaster. Mary tried out for fifth-grade cheerleader at Glenwood Elementary and lost. She was way too uncoordinated for the gymnastics squad. She was even cut from the school glee club – and they usually accepted everyone.

"Don't get your hopes up," Gwen said. "I don't think there's much chance of any of us getting cast in this production."

Mary nibbled on one fingernail as she remembered her mother's words to her that morning. "I want you to be with me, honey, but if you can't fit in here, maybe it's better for you to be with your dad in Oklahoma."

She loved her father, but wasn't too keen about his new wife. More than anything she wanted to stay with her mother. This audition was her last chance.

"I just *have* to be in this ballet!" Mary said with new boldness. "That's all there is to it!"

Courtney Clay, standing by the piano, overheard Mary and laughed out loud. "You'll be lucky if they let you out of the dressing room!"

"I-I don't get it," Mary stammered.

Another girl, wearing the exact same leotard and tights as Courtney, leaned forward. "It's like this," the girl said. "The audition notice said, *dancers*."

"And that means people who can walk across a room without falling down," Courtney finished.

The girls around Courtney burst into laughter at her last words.

Mary felt like she'd been slapped in the face. She stared at the floor trying hard not to cry.

"Hey, you!" a voice rang out. It was Rocky. She pushed back the sleeves of her red satin jacket and marched right up to the sleek Courtney Clay.

Courtney looked at Rocky coolly. "Yes?"

"Leave her alone," Rocky growled. "Or I'll rearrange your face."

For a second Courtney turned completely white. Then she tried to recover, saying, "Ha. Ha. Very funny."

Rocky lowered her voice and hissed, "I'm not kidding."

She strolled back to her new friends, muttering. "Who does that creep think she is, anyway?"

"That's Courtney Clay," Zan whispered. "She's one of Miss Jo's favorites. In point of fact, she's the best dancer of all the sixth-graders."

"Big deal," McGee said, stepping forward. "Does she know how to play ice hockey? No."

"Can she play the piano?" Gwen asked, bringing up her one true talent. "No."

"Has she read *Romeo and Juliet* or *Jane Eyre* or all of the Tiffany Truenote mysteries?" Zan joined in.

"No!" Rocky slammed her fist in her hand. "That's because she's just a Bunhead."

"A what?" Mary Bubnik giggled.

"A Bunhead!" Rocky grinned. "Look at her over there, with her hair pulled tight on the top of her head. And her friends, too. They're just a bunch of Bunheads."

"Bunheads, huh?" Gwen smiled at Rocky and chuckled. "That's a good one."

That moment the door swung open and in stepped Miss Jo and Mr. Anton, who was carrying a clipboard.

He stepped to the front of the classroom and cleared his throat. "First of all, I would like to thank all of you for coming to the auditions this year."

Mary Bubnik's last bit of hope left her. Those were the words that usually led into, "We're very sorry that we can't use everyone..." She stared at the floor and waited to be told to leave.

"I must say, we were a little disappointed in the turn-out," he added, "but because of that, we are pleased to announce that each and everyone of you will be in the show."

Mary Bubnik felt a wave of relief wash over her. Her mother would be so proud that she had finally succeeded at something. The Bunheads hugged each other happily while several of the other girls cheered about the news. The noise was so loud that Mr. Anton didn't hear the groan that came from Rocky, Gwen, Zan and McGee.

"Quiet, please," he demanded and the room fell silent. "Of course, it was difficult to decide which girls should play which parts."

Mary smiled at her new friends. Everything would be just perfect if they could be in the same group.

"Well, maybe we'll get to wear a pretty costume," Gwen said, resigning herself to being in the ballet.

"Yeah," Rocky chimed in. "Long pink tutus for the flower dance."

"I wouldn't mind being a party guest," Zan added. "They wear those old-fashioned dresses with lots of ruffles."

Mr. Anton read off some names. "Mary Bubnik – "

"That's me!" Mary shouted, hopping up and down.

"Gwendolyn Hays, Rochelle Garcia, Suzannah Reed and ... "

He paused just long enough to make McGee get nervous. If she had to be in a ballet, she at least wanted to be with girls she knew.

"Oh, yes, one more." Mr. Anton arched an eyebrow. "Kathryn McGee."

"Well, that's a relief!" Mary Bubnik said. "At least we're all together."

"I can't think of a better group to be laughed off the stage with," Gwen cracked.

"There's definitely safety in numbers," Zan whispered.

"Wait a minute," Rocky said suddenly. "We don't even know what we're playing."

"Yes, are we the flowers?" Gwen asked eagerly, "Or dolls?"

"Or guests?" Zan added.

Mr. Anton looked at Miss Jo and then back at the girls. "None of those."

"What do you mean?" Rocky asked. "What else is there."

"The mice."

"Mice?" all the girls shouted.

"Yes," Mr. Anton explained, "Miss Jo and I talked it over and she felt, after seeing your audition, that – "

"We should play the rats," Rocky finished sarcastically.

"Exactly." Mr. Anton shook his head. "No, no, I mean, mice. We refer to them as mice."

The girls were so stunned by the news, they barely listened as Mr. Anton assigned the flowers to the Bunheads. Courtney and her friends squealed with delight.

"For the time being, the company will rehearse separately," Mr. Anton announced. "They will join us in the final week."

"Who's the company?" Mary whispered to Zan.

"The Cavalier, Clara, Sugar Plum Fairy – "

"Oh, I get it," Mary said. "They dance all of the juicy parts."

"So we'll see you next Saturday, after Thanksgiving, for our first rehearsal." Miss Jo led them all in a final curtsy. "Guests and dolls in the morning at ten o'clock. Flowers and mice at two in the afternoon. Thank you, ladies."

There was an explosion of sound as most of the girls raced for the dressing room.

47

"Well," McGee said with a shrug, "like coach says – you win a few and you lose a few."

"And in point of fact," Zan added, "we didn't exactly lose."

"We just didn't win," Gwen finished.

Mary Bubnik beamed at her new friends. "At least we're all in the same group. As far as I'm concerned, that's more important."

"That's truly true," Zan nodded.

"What are you guys, cheerleaders or something?" Rocky demanded.

"Not me," Mary Bubnik replied. After a second she confessed, "I placed last in my school's cheerleader tryouts."

"Don't feel bad," Gwen said, smiling at Mary. "Whenever people choose up sides, I'm always the last to be picked." Gwen's eyes suddenly widened. She had never told that to a soul before.

"I'm always stuck in the back for class pictures," Zan admitted. "Because I'm so tall." It was a sore spot with Zan, but now it didn't seem so awful.

McGee grinned. "I always have to kneel in the front."

"They don't even let me in the picture," Rocky cracked.

By the time the girls got into the dressing room, the Bunheads had already finished changing and were out in the lobby. Gwen and the gang listened to their laughing, high-pitched voices as they shared the good news with their mothers.

"Forget 'em," Rocky said, "They're just a bunch of show-offs."

"Twinkie, anyone?" Gwen said, digging into her dance bag and passing the spongy cakes around. "All that exercise has made me hungry."

"Why, thank you!" Mary Bubnik took a bite.

Gwen decided, rather than take off her leotard and risk further embarrassment, she would just throw her sweat suit on over her leotard and tights. But she still stepped behind the full-length mirror.

McGee pulled on her jeans, sweatshirt, and denim jacket. Then she leaned against the dressing table, chewing the remainder of Gwen's Twinkie.

"Oh, no, I just thought of something horrible," McGee said with her mouth full.

"What?" Gwen peered out from behind the mirror.

"Our mothers." McGee's eyes were two huge green circles.

"What about them?" Rocky let her hair down and shook it briskly so it stuck out in all directions.

McGee swallowed hard. "How are we going to break it to them that their daughters are going to be up there – "

"In front of a sea of strange faces," Zan cut in.

"Not floating around in beautiful costumes," Mary Bubnik added.

"But looking like jerks in ugly rat suits."

Rocky's final words left everyone so depressed that they walked out of the dressing room in complete silence.

When they got to the bottom of the Hillberry Hall's one hundred and two steps, their mothers were there waiting. Mary Bubnik ran across the street to her car. "See y'all next week!"

Rocky shuffled down the street toward the city bus stop. The last words her new friends heard were, "Don't count on it!"

Chapter Six

The following Saturday was Mrs. Hays' turn to drive the girls to ballet. McGee waited anxiously for the white Cadillac to appear on the road leading to her farmhouse.

McGee couldn't believe that she was actually looking forward to seeing Gwen, but she was. All week long she had thought about their adventure at the audition and their new friends, Rocky, Zan, and Mary Bubnik. Gwen had been pretty clever at the dance studio. McGee never noticed before how funny she could be. Of course, until now, she had tried her hardest to ignore Gwen. That, McGee realized, was her mother's fault for trying to force them to become friends.

Mrs. Hays maneuvered her Cadillac into the gravel drive and honked twice. McGee raced out the front door of her farmhouse. The girls greeted each other with big smiles, but quickly dropped them. Neither one wanted Mrs. Hays to get overly excited about their budding friendship. That would ruin it. Leaning back against the powder-blue seat, both girls played it cool and rode the rest of the way in comfortable silence.

"We're here a half hour early," Mrs. Hays said as she pulled up to the curb in front of Hillberry Hall. "I want to catch the after-Thanksgiving sales. Why don't you go up and wait in the ballet studio?" Her eyes brightened. "You could watch the other dancers rehearse! I bet that'd be exciting."

McGee and Gwen stared at her from the back-seat. Gwen shrugged and nudged McGee to open the door. "Okay, Mom."

"Have fun!" her mother called as she pulled away from the curb.

"So now what do we do?" Gwen asked, shifting her lumpy dance bag under her arm. They looked up at the big granite building and without thinking, they both stuck out their tongues. "The last thing I want to do is go in there *early*," Gwen muttered.

McGee agreed. She pointed across the street at a little red-and-white sign hanging above the entrance to a small restaurant.

"Hi Lo's Pizza and Chinese Food To Go," Gwen said, reading the sign out loud. "Strange."

"I don't see anything else around," McGee said.

"I *am* a little hungry," Gwen admitted. "Let's go."

A bell above the glass door tinkled as they stepped into the tiny place. There was one booth against the back wall. Six round stools, covered in torn and faded red leather, lined a curved counter. An old Chinese man stood behind the counter, engrossed in a small book. A pair of wire-rimmed glasses rested on the tip of his nose.

"You have reservations?" he asked, without looking up.

"Reservations?" Gwen repeated. "There's no one in – "

"I'm sure I can fit you in, no problem," the old man said, his eyes sparkling. He patted the counter in front of him and grinned. "Best seats in the house are right here."

McGee laughed and hopped onto one of the empty stools. Gwen climbed up beside her and surveyed the menu tacked on the wall above the grill.

"What can I get you?" the old man asked as he set paper placemats in front of the girls. "The Hi Lo Special is very good today."

"Hi Lo?" Gwen raised one eyebrow. "Is that your real name?"

The man nodded.

McGee giggled. "You mean, when people see you on the street, they say, Hi, Hi?"

"Exactly."

This tickled Gwen and McGee so much they couldn't stop laughing. Fortunately, Mr. Lo seemed to find his name as funny they did. He waited patiently until they had calmed down enough to give their order.

"I guess it's too early to order pizza," Gwen said half-jokingly to McGee.

"If we eat pizza and then dance, we'll probably throw up." McGee wrinkled her nose. "Coach says you should always wait an hour after you eat before doing anything."

"I thought that was just if you went swimming."

"No, it's with any strenuous exercise."

"Strenuous?" Gwen laughed out loud. "The Rat Dance?" She suddenly gasped. "You don't really think our dance will be hard, do you?"

McGee shrugged. "Could be. How should I know?"

Gwen nervously chewed her lower lip. She had spent the entire week getting used to the idea of standing in front of people in a rat costume. It hadn't even occurred to her that she might really have to *dance*, too.

"I'll have a chocolate shake," Gwen announced. "Extra thick."

"A chocolate shake?" McGee said. "That's as bad as a pizza!"

"I don't care." Gwen folded her arms in front of her. "If this dance is hard, I'm going to need all my strength."

"Hmm, that's true." McGee pursed her lips. The thought of ice cream was beginning to sound very appetizing. "We don't know how long this thing is going to last and I had lunch *hours* ago."

"Me, too," Gwen said. Actually, only an hour before she had consumed two turkey sandwiches and a cup of tomato soup.

"I'll have a chocolate shake, too." McGee decided. "And what the coach doesn't know won't hurt him."

After Mr. Lo had moved away to prepare their order, Gwen asked, "What coach are you talking about?"

"Bill Briggs. He coaches our hockey team, the Fairborn Express."

"You're on that team?" Gwen blinked in disbelief. "I thought that was for boys."

"Nope." McGee smiled proudly. "I'm the first girl." She slumped over the counter. "Or I was."

"Was? Did he kick you off?"

"No, but he probably will. I've already missed one practice because of this dumb ballet."

Gwen was impressed. McGee was a member of the hottest team around, and she didn't even brag about it. Gwen was beginning to like McGee more and more.

Moments later, Mr. Lo appeared with two gigantic frosted glasses filled with ice cream. "Here you go. Two chocolate shakes."

Gwen stabbed hers with a straw and took a deep drink. "Mmmm, this is delicious!"

"Thank you." Mr. Lo beamed. "It's my secret ingredient."

"What secret ingredient?" McGee asked.

He leaned forward and whispered, "Peanut butter."

"Peanut butter!" McGee burst out. "With chocolate? That's too weird."

"Only to you," Mr. Lo chuckled. "To me, it's delicious."

"It sure is," Gwen murmured, as she sipped on her straw. With her other hand she reached for McGee's shake. "I'll drink yours if you don't want it."

"Geez Louise, Gwen!" McGee grabbed her glass and pulled it out Gwen's range. "Give me some time."

"Try it," Mr. Lo encouraged.

McGee took a cautious sip. Then a long slurp. "Hey, it's great!" McGee shook her head in amazement. "It's the best shake I've ever had."

"Good, good." Mr. Lo nodded his head with satisfaction. "See what you might have missed?

It's an old Chinese proverb: Never judge a shake by its secret ingredient."

Mr. Lo turned his attention back to his book while the girls concentrated on their shakes. Gwen slurped up the last drop with her straw, then turned to face McGee. "Tell him your mom made you do it."

"What?" McGee looked up, confused. "Who?"

"Your coach. Tell him your mom forced you to be in the ballet. He can't kick you off the team for something that's not your fault."

"Gwen, are you nuts? I could never do that!"

"Why not? It makes perfect sense to me."

"For one thing, if any of the guys knew I was in a ballet, they'd call me a wimp." McGee shuddered at the thought. "I'd be laughed right off the team."

"Really?" Gwen asked.

"You'd better believe it," McGee said flatly. "No way am I going to let them tease me like that."

"Oh, it's not so bad," Gwen said with a shrug. "You get over it. People have been making fun of me my whole life. First, for being a know-it-all, then for being a *fat* know-it-all." Gwen paused for a moment. "On second thought, forget what I said. It's *worse* than bad, and you *never* get over it."

"That's what I thought," McGee said. The two girls slumped down on their stools, depressed.

"Excuse me?" a voice called gently from the other end of the counter. Gwen and McGee looked up to find Mr. Lo waving at them. "Sorry to intrude.

I couldn't help overhearing your conversation, and I must correct one thought."

"What thought?" McGee asked.

"About dancers being soft," Mr. Lo said. "They are athletes, and anyone who thinks otherwise is very much mistaken."

"I don't understand," Gwen said.

"Well, what does a dancer do?"

McGee stared at the old man as if he were crazy. "A dancer, uh . . . just *dances,* I guess."

"How?"

"What is this, Twenty Questions?" Gwen protested.

"No, please, I'm just curious. What does a dancer do?"

"They jump around a lot," Gwen offered.

"Which takes strong legs, right?"

"And the boy dancers sometimes lift the ballerinas up over their heads," McGee added.

Mr. Lo nodded. "Weight lifting. What else?"

"Ballerinas twirl around and around on their toes," Gwen added.

"Perfect balance," Mr. Lo ticked off the list on his fingers. "And in a ballet, they dance for several hours, right?"

The girls nodded.

Mr. Lo shook his head. "I must be missing something. Here we have a dancer, who must have great strength, balance and agility, plus the endurance of a marathon runner – and your friends say this athlete is a sissy?"

"Well," McGee stammered. "No one's ever actually said anything like that."

"Do *you* think dancers are sissies?"

"No, but I've never heard them called athletes before," Gwen said.

Mr. Lo smiled. "Many high jumpers, divers, figure skaters – even football players – study ballet to become better at their own sport."

"Really?" McGee asked.

He nodded. "Balance, strength, agility. Tell your teammates that ballet is just part of your training."

"What a great idea!" McGee spirits began to soar. "If Coach Briggs thinks I'm doing this for the team, maybe he won't kick me off."

Gwen sat quietly, a smile on her face. "I'm an athlete."

She liked the sound of that. *Athlete.*

McGee looked up at the clock shaped like a dragon and shouted, "Geez Louise! We've got five minutes until rehearsal starts. We'd better run." She leaped up from the counter.

Gwen finished off the rest of McGee's shake with one big gulp. "How much is the bill?"

"For you? The Hi Lo 'Today Only' Special price – free!"

"Gee, thanks!" Gwen said. "We'll come back again."

"And bring our friends," McGee called from the door.

Mr. Lo waved good-bye. "You'd better! Otherwise I won't have any business."

"Bye, Hi!" Gwen yelled as they dashed out the door. That made her start laughing again.

McGee felt so good that she shouted, "Run, run, leap!" all the way up the marble steps.

They were both breathless and giddy by the time they skipped through the door of the Deerfield Academy of Dance. Miss Delacorte waved her long purple scarf at them from behind her desk and they waved back. They couldn't wait to tell the others about Mr. Hi Lo.

McGee threw back the curtain leading to the dressing room and found herself nose-to-nose with Courtney Clay.

"Well, if it isn't the rat pack," Courtney said evenly. She smiled back at two of her friends standing by the mirror. They were making last minute adjustments to their hair, smoothing it into tightly rolled, absolutely perfect buns.

One of them, Page Tuttle, said, "Where are the rest of the rats?"

Before Gwen could snap off a reply, Zan and Mary Bubnik appeared.

"Hi, y'all!" Mary Bubnik chirped. "I'm so glad you're here. Zan and I were afraid it was going to be just us." Mary Bubnik peeked around the coat-rack in the dressing room. "Hey, where's Rocky?"

"I think she skipped out on us," Gwen said, hurrying behind the mirror to change her clothes.

"I thought as much," Zan said. "After Rocky's farewell last week, I was positively positive we'd never see her again." She carefully closed the new book she'd begun and slipped it into her dance bag.

"One down, four to go." Alice Wescott, the whiny fourth grader, smirked from behind the rest of the Bunheads.

"What's that supposed to mean?" McGee challenged.

Alice's courage immediately dissolved, and she turned to the other girls for help.

Page traced her mouth with pink lipstick and said, "The Academy is for serious dancers ONLY."

Courtney nodded. "Rocky didn't belong here and neither do any of you."

Gwen hopped out from behind the mirror. One of her feet was still caught in the leg of her sweatpants. "What do you guys know?" she hissed. "You're just a bunch of Bunheads. We, however, are *athletes.*"

With a satisfied smile, Gwen turned and promptly tripped over her sweatpants. She tumbled awkwardly to the floor, and the Bunheads burst out laughing. Mary Bubnik and McGee rushed to help Gwen to her feet.

"She's so fat, she can't even stand up," Page Tuttle whispered so the whole dressing room could hear.

Zan's eyes blazed with fury. "Page Tuttle, that is the snottiest, snobbiest thing I've ever heard!"

McGee added, "And if you open your mouth again you may find a fist in it."

"Aw, come on, don't fight," Mary Bubnik pleaded. "We're all in this together."

"We'll see how long that lasts," Courtney said coolly. "I'll bet you don't make it to the perform-ance. Any of you."

Courtney flipped the curtain back to leave the dressing room and stopped in her tracks. In the reception hall a man in a dark military uniform was speaking intently with Miss Delacorte. He was wearing a black beret and a shiny silver badge with the Flying Eagle insignia. One of his hands rested firmly on the shoulder of a grim-looking girl.

"Security police," McGee whispered in awe. "They had to arrest Rocky to bring her in."

"I wonder what she did," Zan murmured. "It must have been horribly serious."

Gwen finally untangled her foot from her pants and called out sweetly, "Oh, Courtney. Why don't you tell Rocky what you said about her?"

Courtney didn't answer. She swallowed hard and hurried off toward the rehearsal studio with Page and Alice scurrying along behind her.

The moment they were safely out of range Alice hissed in Rocky's direction, "Juvenile delinquent!"

The security policeman released Rocky and left. Rocky strolled casually into the dressing room.

"Boy, are we glad to see you!" Mary Bubnik said.

"You are?" Rocky looked up in surprise. A pleased half-smile crept across her lips.

"You wouldn't believe what just happened," Gwen said. She told Rocky about their encounter with the Bunheads, leaving out the part where Page had called her fat. She couldn't bring herself to repeat it, especially after she had just eaten a Hi Lo Special chocolate shake.

"Are you kidding me?" Rocky angrily tossed her red satin jacket onto a bench. "Boy, those Bunheads are cruisin' for a bruisin'." She tugged her wild hair roughly into a ponytail. "We'll show them!"

"Excuse me, girls." Miss Delacorte peeked through the curtain. "The mice will be rehearsing in Studio A and the flowers in Studio B." She clapped her hands together. "Hurry, hurry, you mustn't be late."

Everyone grabbed their dance bags and filed out of the dressing room. As they stepped through the door into Studio A, McGee grabbed Rocky's arm and whispered, "I can't believe the police had to arrest you to get you here. That really scared the Bunheads!"

Rocky cocked her head. "What are you talking about?"

"The security policeman talking to Miss Delacorte. He looked really mean."

Rocky rolled her eyes at McGee. "That's my dad. He always looks like that."

"Then why were you late?" McGee asked.

"We got caught in traffic."

"But I thought you were going to skip."

A huge grin covered Rocky's face. "What? And miss another action-packed day with you guys? Never." With that, Rocky strutted over to the piano and plopped her bag on top of it. "Let's dance."

Chapter Seven

"Remember, keep your hands fluttering in front of your face," Miss Jo reminded the girls as she ran them through the steps for the mouse dance. "Like little whiskers."

"That's the easy part," Mary Bubnik whispered to Gwen.

"And keep your *jeté* high and clean," Miss Jo called out.

"That's the hard part," Gwen grumbled as she struggled to keep up.

McGee did a couple of *jetés* in a circle, leaping as high as she could. "Don't forget," she said to Gwen, "you're an athlete. Strong and powerful."

"Right. I'm an athlete." Gwen threw herself into the next *jeté*. She landed with a thud and caught a glimpse of herself in the mirror with her stomach sticking out. "That's a laugh."

"No, no, Mary Bubnik," Miss Jo called out. "Turn to the left, not to the right."

Mary Bubnik grinned, turned to the left and promptly ran into Zan, who was trying not to draw any attention to herself.

"Sorry," she apologized.

"It's all right," Zan whispered. "Stay in front of me, OK? It's almost over."

The girls ran a ragged circle, then burst apart on Miss Jo's command. As they went into their final leaps, Rocky and McGee's *grand jetés* were extra high. Rocky even threw in a karate kick and yell.

Mrs. Bruce hit one last resounding chord and Miss Jo clapped her hands. "That was a very good start. So much enthusiasm is nice to see!"

McGee gave Rocky a high five. Gwen and Mary Bubnik grinned at each other. Even Zan felt a little encouraged.

"Gather around me in a circle on the floor, girls," Miss Jo instructed. "Now that you know the steps to the dance – "

"Who said we know the steps?" Mary Bubnik asked, wide-eyed. She was having trouble remembering whether it was two *jetés* and a run, run, run, or three.

Miss Jo smiled and continued. "It is important to know the story of your part in the ballet. Then we can add the acting, which is as important to the performance of this dance as the steps."

"Oh, great," Gwen grumbled to Rocky. "First she tells me I have to dance. Now I have to act? If singing is included in all of this, you can count me out."

Rocky gave Gwen a swift jab in the side. "I like acting."

"So?" Gwen blinked at her. "I don't."

"Shhh!" Zan put her finger to her lips. She knew the story by heart but she was eager to hear Miss Jo tell it.

"You all remember that Clara was given a magical Nutcracker at the Christmas Party?"

The five girls nodded.

"Well, after the party," Miss Jo began, "at the stroke of midnight a magic spell takes hold of the entire household." She lowered her voice dramatically. "That's when the Mouse King gathers his evil forces."

"That must be us!" Mary Bubnik sang out.

"That's right." Miss Jo leaned forward. "At first you are just a haunting whisper rustling in the shadows."

Outside, the sun went behind a cloud and the room darkened for a fraction of a second. Without thinking, Zan and Mary Bubnik shivered.

"Then the mice become a terrifying force, an army of the night," Miss Jo continued.

Rocky whispered, "I like that."

"From every corner of the old mansion, you come creeping and scurrying, getting ready for battle."

The girls leaned forward, hanging on Miss Jo's every word. Her voice fell to a whisper. "At first your movements are tiny. *Jeté, jeté,* and run, run, run." She demonstrated with her long hands.

"Then the Nutcracker appears, and you show your power." Miss Jo's voice grew stronger and the girls sat up straight. "Violent movements. *Grand jetés.* We want to scare the Nutcracker and his army, so our movements are ungraceful and grotesque. No pointed toes."

"That's a relief," Mary Bubnik said. "When I point my toes, these big old shoes of mine always flop off."

"And your expressions are frightening, like a creature from a nightmare," Miss Jo added. She made a face at them, and the girls all laughed.

"Geez Louise," McGee chuckled, "this could be fun."

Zan kept quiet. It didn't sound like fun to her. The fact of the matter was, she would still have to get up in front of all those people and make a fool of herself.

"Now, let's try the dance again," Miss Jo announced. "Only this time, try to act your parts. Think like mice, *be* mice."

She was interrupted by a stirring at the door. The gang looked up to see Courtney and Page peeking around the corner, wide grins on their faces. Alice Wescott and few of the other Bunheads were grouped behind them in the hall.

"Oh, great!" Gwen muttered to McGee. "You don't think they saw us rehearsing, do you?"

"I hope not," Zan whispered back. "We'll never hear the end of it."

"Come in, come in!" Miss Jo waved the girls into the room. "Mr. Anton's group will be joining us for the final part of our rehearsal," She explained to the mice.

"Perfect," Gwen groaned. "Just perfect!"

Mr. Anton stepped into the studio, followed by a dark-haired boy with electric blue eyes. Gwen and Mary Bubnik gasped out loud.

"Who's the hunk?" Rocky asked out of the corner of her mouth.

A dreamy look filled Zan's eyes. "That's Derek McClellan. He dances the Cavalier in the ballet. Isn't he beautiful?"

Mary Bubnik sighed. "Gorgeous!"

"That does it!" Gwen sucked in her stomach. "I'm starting my diet tomorrow."

A few more dancers from the ballet company filed into the room. Mr. Anton conferred with Miss Jo for a few moments, then turned to the group. "I know it is just the first rehearsal, but I would like to share the progress of our young ballerinas with the rest of the company."

"What's that mean?" Mary Bubnik whispered to Zan.

"I think – in fact, I'm practically certain," Zan said, "that he wants us to do our dance."

"In front of him?" Gwen pointed at Derek McClellan, who was leaning easily against the dance barre.

"In front of everybody," Rocky said.

"I couldn't," Gwen said, shaking her head. "I'd die!"

McGee glanced at the clock. "Ten minutes left of rehearsal. If we're lucky, they won't get to us."

That hope was snuffed out as Courtney raised her hand. "Mr. Anton, you really should watch the mice first." She flashed the gang a sickeningly sweet smile. "They've worked so hard this afternoon."

"She's right," Gwen blurted out. "We've worked so hard, we're exhausted."

Mr. Anton chuckled, then turned to Courtney. "That's very gracious of you, Miss Clay. I think that's a wonderful idea."

"But Mr. Anton," Mary Bubnik drawled, "I'm sure the flowers' dance must be beautiful. If they went first – "

"It would truly inspire us," Zan finished.

McGee kept her eye glued to the clock. "Keep

stalling," she whispered under her breath to Rocky. "Just a few more minutes and we'll be out of here."

Rocky was too busy glaring at Courtney to hear.

"Come along, girls," Miss Jo said briskly, "this is no time to be shy."

Rocky broke the silence. "Hey, it's just a dance," she said casually. "No big deal."

She stood up and walked over to the corner to take her position. As she passed Courtney, Rocky hissed, "One more strike and you're out. Remember that."

Courtney stared back at Rocky, a tiny smile curling the edges of her mouth.

The others hurried to join Rocky. As they waited for the music to begin, Mary Bubnik repeated over and over, "Please let me get through this without falling. Please! Oh, please! Oh, please!"

Miss Bruce hit the chords that sounded like a clock ringing the hour. At the final stroke of midnight, McGee led the others into their first step of the dance.

What followed was total disaster. Gwen, who was right behind McGee, started too soon and then had to stop abruptly to get back in rhythm. Rocky and Zan promptly crashed into her back.

Courtney and the rest of the Bunheads started giggling. A couple of the other dancers burst out laughing. To her horror, Gwen noticed that even Derek McClellan was grinning.

Hearing the laughter made Rocky furious. She broke out of the line and started doing karate kicks in their direction. Meanwhile, Mary Bubnik, who still couldn't remember any of the steps, decided just to follow Rocky and make gruesome faces. Gwen stuck close to McGee but Zan kept sandwiching herself in between them, trying to hide from their audience. The result was that no one could move without tripping over the other.

In a panic, McGee led them into the circle ending the dance long before their cue. The girls had no choice but to keep running around and around, waiting for the music to stop.

Every time Gwen passed by Derek McClellan she tried to suck in her stomach. On the fifth rotation, Gwen suddenly felt the effects of Hi Lo's special shake. Without warning, she was seized with a stomach cramp and bent forward, clutching her sides.

Mary Bubnik tumbled right over Gwen's back and onto the floor.

"I think I'm going to be sick!" Gwen gasped, her face deathly green. She turned and charged for the exit.

"I'll go help her!" McGee bolted out of the room after Gwen.

Gwen raced through the lobby of the Academy with one hand clapped over her mouth. She barely made it into the bathroom. Leaping inside, she slammed the door behind her and locked it.

McGee raced to the bathroom door. Behind her she could hear the final chords of their music and then silence.

"Gwen, come out of that bathroom," McGee shouted through the locked door. "You can't stay in there forever."

"Watch me," Gwen shot back. Then she whispered, "Is rehearsal over yet?"

McGee turned and watched the dancers pouring out of the studio. "Yes, it is."

"Has he gone?"

"Who?"

"What do you mean, who?" Gwen barked. "Derek McClellan. The dancing hunk, who just witnessed the most embarrassing moment of my entire life."

"We all embarrassed ourselves," McGee reminded her.

"Then go find your own place to hide. This one is taken."

McGee heaved a huge sigh. "Come on out, Gwen, please?"

Gwen didn't respond. McGee saw Rocky, Zan, and Mary Bubnik coming toward her through the lobby.

"Is she OK?" Zan asked, her eyes full of concern.

"Yes, but she won't come out," McGee said. "She's too embarrassed."

"You think she's embarrassed?" Mary Bubnik moaned. "You should have been with us for the big finale." She leaned against the wall. "Boy, was my face red!"

"What did Mr. Anton say?" McGee asked.

"Not much," Zan said. "He just kind of stared at us for a while."

"And he wasn't smiling," Rocky added. Her mouth set in a hard line as she said, "But the Bunheads were."

"Gwen?" Mary Bubnik tapped lightly on the bathroom door.

"Go away."

"Now, there's no use staying in there," Mary said through the door. "Sooner or later, you're going to have to come out."

"Never."

"Well, what are you going to do in there?"

"I'll probably waste away for a week or so, then keel over dead from starvation."

Rocky shouted over Mary's shoulder, "You'll probably die of boredom first."

"Let me try," Zan stepped up to the door. "Gwen, this is Zan. I know how awfully awful you must feel, but it's not your fault."

"It's the Bunheads' fault!" Rocky declared.

"That's exactly correct," Zan said.

Mary Bubnik leaned forward and whispered, "If you're worried about that gorgeous guy seeing you embarrass yourself – well, he didn't."

"How do you know?"

"Because when I hit the floor, I caught a glimpse of him reading a magazine."

"What?" Gwen's voice was filled with outrage. "You mean we killed ourselves, acting and dancing our brains out, and he didn't even have the courtesy to watch?"

"That's right, Gwen," McGee said.

The bathroom door flew open and hit the wall with a thunk. "I'll show him. I'll show them all."

"That's more like it!" Rocky narrowed her eyes. "And we'll start with the Bunheads."

Gwen stepped into the lobby and faced the rest of the gang. "We've got to think of a way to get back at them."

"Like putting lead weights in their flowers?" Rocky suggested. "Or maybe pins in their ballet shoes?"

Zan shook her head. "No, it has to be something wickedly clever."

"Well, what, then?" Rocky demanded.

"I don't know," Zan admitted. "But we've got a whole week to plan."

"That's right," McGee said with a grin. "And among the five of us, we should be able to think of something *good*."

Chapter Eight

Once she got home from rehearsal, Zan decided to go to the park near her parents' apartment and finish her latest Tiffany Truenote mystery. She was right in the middle of the final chapter when an idea came to her.

"That's it!" she said. "The way to get back at the Bunheads is to let them get themselves!"

Tossing the book aside, she dug into her book bag and pulled out a sheet of paper filled with names and phone numbers. It listed everyone who was involved in *The Nutcracker*.

"Contact sheet," Zan said out loud, reading the words written across the top. She decided it was time to make contact.

Zan raced across the park back to her apartment building and ran up the stairs to the third floor. Her parents, who were both artists and taught at the Deerfield Art Institute, had converted the entire floor into an open loft apartment. The walls were covered with original paintings and textured wall hangings. Zan opened the door with her key and hurried past the paintings to her room.

Though the rest of the apartment was decorated in an ultra-modern style, Zan had insisted on having an old-fashioned bedroom. Her bed was made of polished brass and covered with a quilted comforter. Little lace pillows were neatly arranged along the headboard.

Zan sprawled across the bed and studied her contact sheet for a moment. She picked up the phone on her nightstand and dialed Mary Bubnik's number. Mary lived in Glenwood, right on the edge of Deerfield, so Zan figured she would have gotten home from rehearsal first.

The phone rang three times before a breathless voice answered. "Bubnik household, Mary speaking."

"Mary, this is Zan Reed."

"Oh, hi!" Zan heard some mumblings on Mary's end and Mary's voice saying, "It's my friend Zan from ballet."

Finally Mary came back on the line. "I wish you could see my mother's face right now," she whispered. "She is just thrilled that I have a made a new friend here in Deerfield."

Zan giggled. She knew her parents would probably have had the same reaction if Mary had called her.

"What's up?" Mary asked.

"Well, I was pondering our desperate need for a plan while finishing the last chapter of *The Fatal Flaw*, when it hit me." Zan took a deep breath. "Have you ever heard the saying, 'Give them enough rope, and they'll hang themselves'?"

"Yes, I believe I have," Mary Bubnik drawled. "I think it is downright gruesome." Suddenly Mary gasped. "Zan, you don't really want to – ?"

"Oh, no, it just means that if we make the right 'suggestions' to Courtney and the Bunheads, they may just humiliate themselves."

There was a long pause. "I don't think I get you."

It took Zan several minutes to convince Mary to trust her scheme and just follow instructions. But when Zan called McGee, she caught on right away.

"This is great, Zan," McGee chuckled. "What do I need to do?"

"We should each go to the library and check out a couple of books about the history of ballet."

"Got it." McGee made a note to bring a large brown bag to school with her. She'd hide the books in there and that way none of her hockey team-mates would ever see them. McGee had lost the courage to tell her coach about being in ballet, and the last thing she needed was to be caught with a lot of dance books.

"You call Gwen and Rocky and tell them to do the same," Zan continued, "and then we'll all meet at the studio early on Saturday – "

"Before the Bunheads get there," McGee finished for her. "They'll never know what hit them!"

"Right!" Zan hung up the phone, picked up her stuffed brown bear and danced around the bedroom. "Well, Mr. Gallagher," she said to the fuzzy toy. "It looks like we're not alone anymore. We've got some friends. What do you think about that?"

Zan was answered by a gentle knock on her door.

"Zan?" A tall black woman who looked like a grown-up version of Zan stuck her head in the room. "How was ballet rehearsal?"

"Great, Mom!" Zan smiled happily. "I think we're going to win."

Mrs. Reed cocked her head in confusion. "Win? I didn't realize there was a contest involved."

"Neither did we," Zan replied. "Until today."

The following Saturday, the gang came to the studio prepared. Each girl was loaded down with books checked out from her local library. They gathered in a corner of the deserted dressing room and held a hushed meeting.

Zan was delighted to see that everyone had followed her instructions to the letter. "You all look fantastically wonderful!"

McGee had wrapped her braids around her head in a neat crown. She'd even worn a pair of tights without a run in them. Mary's hair was tied in a curly ponytail with a bright blue ribbon.

Gwen's hair was too short to do anything special with it. However, she had removed her thick glasses and the transformation was startling, especially when she managed not to squint.

Rocky was the biggest surprise. She had tamed her wild mane of hair into a taut bun at the base of her neck, just like Miss Jo's. She grinned proudly. "We almost look like real Bunheads." She slipped her red satin jacket on over her leotard. "Almost."

Zan, her own dark hair pulled into a neat bun like the others, said, "What's important is that the Bunheads think we're serious about ballet. Now, the first thing we should do is set the scene." Zan covered the makeup table with ballet books, propping several of them open to specific pages. "Mary, you sit here and pretend to look at the pictures."

Gwen picked up one of the books and leaned against the locker as though she were deep in thought.

"Remember," Zan whispered, "no matter what any of us says, go along with it!"

"Got it!" McGee perched on the edge of the dressing table and pretended to be engrossed in a book of her own.

Rocky, who had moved to the door to keep lookout, whistled softly. Moments later Courtney sailed into the dressing room. Page Tuttle and Alice Wescott followed close behind. Without looking at the gang, the Bunheads went straight to their usual places and began to get dressed for rehearsal.

McGee looked over at Zan and winked. That was their signal to begin.

"Oh, yes," Zan announced loudly, as if she were continuing a previous conversation, "the very, very best dancers *always* use Snowy soap flakes on their shoes, to keep from falling."

"That's amazing," Gwen said. "I thought they used resin, like that stuff over there." She pointed to a little box sitting in the corner of the dressing room. The dancers at the Academy dipped their shoes in its sticky granules to keep from slipping.

Rocky jumped in without missing a beat. "Resin's old hat. All of the really big New York City dancers put Snowy in their resin boxes. It's a well-known secret. In fact, it's so popular that stores have trouble keeping it in stock."

Gwen raised an eyebrow at Rocky, as if to say, "Don't push it."

"It's easy to take care of," Zan added, "and washes right off. It says so right here in *Dance World*

Today." She held up the magazine, flipping it quickly to make sure none of the Bunheads could really see the page.

McGee peeked around the corner of her book to see if Courtney was responding. McGee smiled. Courtney was hanging on to every word they were saying and so was Page Tuttle.

Zan pulled a huge box of Snowy soap flakes out of her back pack. "Here, you guys, I brought this. Feel free to use some."

"Thanks, Zan." Gwen smiled and gestured to her overstuffed pink patent leather bag. "But I already have my own."

"Oooh, look at the way these dancers tie the ribbons on their toe shoes," Mary Bubnik exclaimed, pointing in her book. "Why, they lace them right up to their knees!"

"Of course," Zan said casually. "That's an age-old ballet tradition."

McGee said, "But I thought you were supposed to tie them around your ankles."

Zan shook her head. "That was before. Now all of the really good dancers crisscross them up their legs. You'll notice the dancers in that picture are in *The Nutcracker*."

Mary overacted surprised. "Why, Zan's right! They sure are." She called over her shoulder, "Courtney, these girls are doing the Waltz of the Flowers."

82

"Are they really?" Courtney shrugged, pretending not to care.

"Listen to this!" Gwen pretended to read from her book. "For over a hundred years, the traditions of the ballet have been handed from generation to generation."

She paused to see how her phony speech was going over. McGee gestured for her to keep talking.

"From Pavlova's Dying Swan and the grand tradition of wearing a crown of feathers" – Gwen paused to collect her thoughts – "to the high-laced toe shoe ribbons worn by the ballerinas in the Waltz of the Flowers – the greatness continues!"

The gang turned to look at Courtney, who was taking a *very* long time to adjust her hair in the mirror.

"Boy, I sure envy you guys," Mary Bubnik declared with a loud sigh. "Getting to wear toe shoes and lacing your ribbons up high like that."

"Like real ballerinas," McGee agreed.

Courtney smiled at her reflection in the mirror. They could see she felt flattered.

"Well, maybe someday," Courtney said with a regal wave of her hand, "you, too, will get to wear toe shoes. I wouldn't count on it, though."

Zan nodded sadly. "I guess we'll have to be content to only dream of becoming a *real* ballerina – like you, Courtney." Zan rolled her eyes and McGee had to smother a giggle with her hand.

Courtney did a couple of stretches, aware that she was being watched. She reached gracefully to the ceiling, then bent forward. When her nose touched her knees, she declared, "Practice makes perfect."

"That's true." Rocky motioned for the others to pick up their books and follow her. "Guess we'd better go on into the studio. I sure hope we can squeeze in a little extra practice on our mouse dance."

They walked as casually as they could out of the dressing room and into the studio. Rocky led them to the far side of the classroom where they burst into giggles.

"Do you think the plan will work?" McGee asked, her cheeks flushed with excitement.

"We'll know as soon as we see their toe shoe ribbons," Zan replied.

"If they fall for that," Gwen chortled, "then they'll fall for the soap flakes and put Snowy in the resin box."

"Now, if anything happens," Rocky said quickly, "I want you guys to remember, keep a poker face!"

"A poker face?" Mary Bubnik repeated. "What's that?"

"This." Rocky stared straight ahead without putting any expression on her face. "People do it when they play cards," she explained. "That way no one can guess what they're thinking or what cards they have in their hands."

They all faced the large mirror and tried out various blank expressions.

There was a sudden commotion at the door to the studio and a jumble of voices could be heard outside.

Miss Jo and Mrs. Bruce entered the room first, followed by Mr. Anton and various members of the ballet company.

"All right, we have a lot to do today, and very little time," Mr. Anton announced. "So we will go through the dances one by one, beginning with the Waltz of the Flowers."

Miss Jo clapped her hands. "Dancers, take your positions please!"

The dancers of the *corps de ballet* of the Academy consisted of twelve girls in their late teens. They were to be joined in the Waltz of the Flowers by the younger dancers, led by Courtney Clay.

"Cross your fingers, everybody," Gwen whispered. "Here come the Bunheads!"

First the older girls waltzed in a line across the room. Then came Courtney, smiling beautifully as she danced.

The first sign of anything unusual was the trail of white footprints left behind her as she crossed the studio floor.

Snickers went around the room as other dancers noticed the pretty pink satin ribbons she had carefully wrapped around her calves up to her knee.

Behind her, Page and Alice and few of the other Flowers had done the same.

McGee jabbed Gwen in the side. "It worked!"

"Shhh!" Rocky hushed her. The five girls sat quietly in their corner and waited for the fun to begin.

More and more white footprints appeared until soon the wooden floor was almost covered with them.

"Uh-oh," Rocky whispered as the girls doubled back for a diagonal cross. "Here it comes."

Page leaped out confidently. The foot she landed on hit the white flakes and shot out from under her. She reached out blindly and clutched at Courtney's arm. The two of them collapsed in a heap, just as the rest of the girls began to slip and slide behind them.

Mrs. Bruce stopped playing. Several of the older dancers rushed onto the floor to help the girls. Within seconds they were flailing around helplessly. No one could get enough traction to stand up.

"Wowie!" was all McGee could say.

"They look like skaters in slow motion," Gwen whispered.

"I hope no one's hurt," Mary Bubnik said.

"Naw." Rocky shook her head. "Just surprised."

Finally one of the girls crawled on her hands and knees to the *barre* and pulled herself up to a standing position. One by one the others did the same.

Within minutes order had returned to the room and a furious Mr. Anton turned to Courtney and her companions.

"What is the meaning of this?" he demanded. "What have you put on your shoes?"

One of the older dancers touched the white powder on the floor and rubbed her fingers. "I think this is soap."

"Soap!" Mr. Anton turned to Courtney. "What possessed you to put soap on your shoes?"

"I-I'm sorry," Courtney mumbled.

"We thought that – " Page began, then finished lamely, "We didn't know."

Courtney shot an angry look at the gang. Rocky hissed, "Poker face!"

Immediately they stared straight ahead. Not a glimmer of emotion showed on their faces.

It was hard. Gwen really wanted to laugh. She bit her cheek, which brought only tears to her eyes.

"And those ribbons! Is this a joke?" Mr. Anton pointed at the laced ribbons that had tumbled down around their ankles. "You shouldn't have toe shoes unless you know how to wear them."

"Anton, I'm sure the girls meant no harm," Miss Jo said, putting her hand on his shoulder to calm him down.

"It's unbelievable," he fumed. "This dance floor is a mess of soap flakes. We can't rehearse here. They have completely ruined our afternoon."

Miss Jo led him over to the piano, gesturing for Courtney and the rest of the Flowers to quietly leave the studio.

"This is everything we could have hoped for," Gwen whispered, "And more."

The Bunheads never came back. Miss Jo took the mice to Studio B and ran through their dance quickly, then dismissed them early.

When the gang left Hillberry Hall, they found an angry Courtney Clay waiting for them on the steps.

"No one, but no one, humiliates Courtney Clay," she hissed through clenched teeth. "You little rats are going to regret this. I mean it."

Before anyone could reply, she stalked off down the steps.

"Boy, oh, boy," Mary Bubnik muttered. "Those sound like fighting words to me."

McGee solemnly faced the group. "I think it's time for a meeting."

Gwen nodded. "At Hi Lo's."

"Where?" Rocky asked.

McGee pointed across the street to the little red-and-white sign. "He's our friend and the food is great."

Gwen instinctively clutched her stomach. "Just be careful of anything with a special ingredient."

Chapter Nine

"Greetings and salutations! Welcome, one and all!" Mr. Lo greeted the girls as they trooped through the door of the tiny restaurant. The bell over the door jingled noisily.

"Hi, Hi!" Gwen shouted.

"Mr. Hi Lo, I'd like you to meet Zan, Rocky, and Mary Bubnik." McGee pointed to each girl as they hopped onto the worn leather stools. "They're friends of ours."

"I am honored, young ladies, that you would grace my humble place of business with your presence." Mr. Lo bowed low, then leaned forward on the counter. "What can I bring you?" he asked.

"Chinese pizza? Italian chow mein?" He winked at Gwen. "Or today's Hi Lo Special?"

"No, no!" she said quickly. "I think everyone just wants a Coke. Right?"

The gang all nodded.

"An excellent choice." Mr. Lo scribbled their order on his pad. "An important meeting should always begin with a shared drink between friends."

"How'd you know we were having a meeting?" Rocky asked as the other girls stared at Mr. Lo in amazement.

"I have my ways," Mr. Lo replied. He pointed at Zan, who had already set a lavender notepad on the counter and carefully written the date and the words, IMPORTANT MEETING, at the top of the page.

Mr. Lo was still grinning when he disappeared into the back of the shop to get their drinks. Zan held her pen poised in her hand, ready to take notes. She looked over at McGee expectantly.

"Okay," McGee began, "the way I see it, the Bunheads have declared war, pure and simple." She looked from one face to the next. "Now we have to decide what to do about it."

Rocky spoke first. "We can't back down. We've got to hang tough and beat 'em." She slammed her fist down hard on the counter.

Gwen swallowed hard. "Are you talking about *real* fighting? The kind where people hit each other with fists and things?"

Rocky shrugged. "It might come to that."

"I'm sorry, you'll have to count me out," Mary Bubnik shook her head. "I am just not the fighting type."

"I don't think any of us *really* are." Zan said. Rocky tensed and Zan added, "What I mean is, I think we are all smarter than that."

Mr. Lo reappeared with a tray. "Here you are, ladies," he announced, setting an icy cold drink in front of each one.

"Thanks, Hi," McGee murmured, taking a sip of her drink.

Noticing their glum faces, he asked, "More ballet troubles?"

Five heads bobbed as one.

"Not your coach again?" he said to McGee. "I thought we took care of that – "

"That's not it," McGee interrupted. She didn't want to admit that she still hadn't told her coach about the ballet. She didn't have the guts to tell him, and now she was starting to lie. That morning she had called in sick, pretending to have laryngitis.

"It's the Bunheads!" Rocky blurted.

"They're out to ruin our lives!" Mary Bubnik declared.

"Bunheads?" Mr. Lo shook his head in confusion.

McGee, happy that the subject had changed, explained, "You know, the girls in ballet class who think they're better than everyone else, and pull their hair into tight little knots on top of their heads."

"Oh, I see! BUN-heads!" Mr. Los' face burst into a smiling sea of tiny wrinkles. "That's a good one! But why would your fellow students cause you trouble?"

"Well, it all started," Gwen explained, "with Courtney Clay – she's their leader, and a real snob."

"She's always saying lousy things about us," Rocky said. "Like we're no good."

"And she's so two-faced about it," Zan complained. "Miss Jo, our teacher, thinks she's sweet because Courtney butters her up." Zan's eyes filled with tears. "Last summer she came up to me and told me I was as ugly as a giraffe. And twice as clumsy."

"WHAT?" McGee exploded. "You never told us that!"

"Oh, Zan, that's awful!" Mary Bubnik put her arm around Zan's shoulder.

Rocky slammed her first into her palm and muttered, "Three strikes, that's it, she's out!"

Gwen looked up at Mr. Lo. "You see what we mean? Last week she and her friends set us up to be made fun of by the whole company."

McGee started to giggle. "We sure got 'em back today!"

Rocky grinned. "Right! Seeing Courtney sliding all over the place was worth anything."

"So you got revenge?" Mr. Lo asked in his quiet voice.

The gang nodded.

"And now you are happy," he continued. "But you don't look happy."

"Courtney said she's going to get us," Zan explained.

"And she will, too," Mary Bubnik said in a scared little voice.

"And then we'll get her back, and her rotten friends twice as bad," Rocky declared. "Right?"

No one answered her. "Right?" she repeated.

"That's just it, Rocky," Gwen said slowly. "We'll get her back, and then the Bunheads will retaliate, and then we'll have to do something else – "

"It could go on forever," McGee said.

Zan slumped down on her stool. "With everybody getting meaner and meaner."

"I never thought about that." Rocky looked from one girl to the other. "So what are we going to do? We can't just sit here and let Courtney have the last word."

There was a long pause.

"Would that be so awful?" Mary Bubnik asked. "I mean, she is more experienced and all."

Gwen burst out, "You mean, admit that the Bunheads are better than us?"

"No way!" McGee shook her head.

"But we can't go on like this," Zan protested. "I think Mary's being sensible."

"Never, never, never!" The look in Rocky's eye made it clear that there was no point in discussing it further.

This time the silence lasted for a whole minute. When Gwen sucked up the last of her Coke with her straw, the sound was so loud, everybody jumped.

"I think you ladies are at what's called an impasse," Mr. Lo said.

Rocky snorted. "If that means we're not getting anywhere, you're right."

"May I make one small suggestion?" the old man asked.

Gwen shrugged. "Sure."

"Perhaps you should try to beat them at their own game."

"You mean ballet?" Gwen asked. "How could we do that?"

"Practice."

It was McGee who had spoken. "Two years ago I had never even ice skated, but with practice – "

"McGee not only learned how to skate, but she was chosen to be on the Fairview Express." Gwen made the announcement proudly, as if it were her own accomplishment.

"Wow! The Fairview Express," Rocky repeated. "That is hot."

Gwen nodded and looped her arm over McGee's shoulder. "That shows you what practice can do."

"That's wonderful, McGee," Zan said. "Maybe, just maybe, if we practiced extra hard, we could do our dance better than the Bunheads."

"Gee, I don't know." Mary Bubnik said. "It sounds like a good idea, but I don't think I can dance any better."

"Sure you can!" McGee encouraged. "You've just had a little trouble with your shoes."

"And memory," Gwen added.

"And sense of direction," Rocky chimed in.

"But it's nothing major," Zan said. "Besides, you have such a wonderful expressive face."

"And it's like Miss Jo said," Rocky declared. "Our dance relies as much on acting as it does on dancing. I could coach us all in scary looks."

"Say, we could hold practice at my house," Gwen piped up. "We've got a big basement. My mom would be thrilled. Plus I make great after-practice snacks."

"Okay!" Zan wrote down "Practice at Gwen's house" on her pad of paper. She looked up at the group. "When?"

"Wednesday, after school," Rocky decided. "That way we can practice on our own for a few days beforehand."

"Anyone have any problems with that?" McGee asked, looking around the group. "Then it's settled."

"I'll give you all my address," Gwen said, scrounging in her dance bag for some paper to write on. The thought of throwing a party really excited her. "And we'll meet as soon as everyone can get there after school."

"My mother would be happy to pick everyone up and drive us over," Mary Bubnik offered.

While the girls exchanged addresses, Gwen made a list out loud. "Let's see, Mom goes to the store on Monday. She'll have to get chips, dip, frozen pizzas, ice cream – maybe some candy bars for extra energy."

McGee looked at her watch and gulped. "Uh-oh, Mom's probably been waiting ten minutes. C'mon, Gwen, we've got to go!"

Everyone jumped up and pulled money out to pay for their Cokes. Mr. Lo, who had gone back to his stool while they were planning, looked up from his newspaper and smiled. "So, did you decide what to do about your problem?"

Gwen nodded happily. "I think we've got it under control."

Rocky slapped McGee on the shoulder. "McGee had the best idea. We're going to out-dance those Bunheads in the ballet. That'll shut 'em up."

"Good!" Mr. Lo exclaimed. "I'm glad you worked it out."

"Me, too!" Zan sighed with relied.

"It was a real pleasure meeting you, Mr. Lo," Mary Bubnik said, going up to him and holding out her hand.

He shook it warmly. "The pleasure was all mine, Mary Bubnik. Are you sure you don't have time for a Hi Lo Special?"

"Run for it, everybody!" Gwen yelled as she dashed for the door. "Bye, Hi!"

Chapter Ten

On Wednesday Gwen could hardly wait for school to get out. As soon as the bell rang, she ran out the main entrance of Brooke Hollow Elementary, feeling as light as a bird. Her mother was waiting for her by the curb in her white Cadillac.

Usually Gwen rode the bus home after school, which was a torture she endured. None of the other kids ever wanted to sit with her, so she usually ended up sitting in the front seat with Freddie Alverson, the bus driver's four-year-old son.

Today, however, was a special occasion. She had four friends coming to her house for a party. "And a short ballet practice," Gwen reminded herself.

"Hurry up, Mom!" Gwen urged as she scooted

into the front seat. "The gang should be arriving any minute, and I need to have all the snacks ready."

Mrs. Hays smiled at her daughter. For four days, Gwen had talked of nothing but the party.

"OK, the first thing we do when everyone gets there is push back the couches in the basement," Gwen said, going over her plan of action. "Then pop the pizzas in the oven." She paused. "No, we'd better put the pizzas in first, then move the couches."

"Don't you worry about a thing," Mrs. Hays told her. "I'll take care of the details. Besides, a good hostess should always greet her guests at the door."

Gwen could tell that her mom was delighted she was entertaining friends from the ballet. For the first time in ages, Gwen felt like she and her mother had something in common. They had spent the last few days actually having fun together. They'd shopped for groceries, baked cookies, and rearranged the furniture in the living room. Mrs. Hays, who normally kept her house sparkling clean, had even hired a person from "Maid in the Shade" to make it look absolutely perfect.

When they pulled into the Hays' driveway, Gwen could hear the phone ringing inside their house. She raced up the sidewalk and ran straight into the kitchen.

"Hello?" Gwen cradled the phone under her chin as she flipped on the switch for the oven.

"Gwen?" A distant, hollow voice echoed in her ear. "It's me, McGee."

"You sound like you're talking in a swimming pool." Gwen pulled two frozen pizzas out of the freezer and peeled off their wrappers.

"Try the Fairview Ice Arena," McGee shouted. "I'm using the phone in Coach Briggs' office."

"What are you doing there?"

"Coach scheduled practice for the Express today. It was a last minute thing."

"What? That's not fair!" Gwen opened the oven as she spoke and slid the pizzas onto the racks. "You just hang up and come here. Tell him we've got dance practice starting in ten minutes."

"I can't." McGee lowered her voice. "I never told him I was in the ballet."

"Why not?"

"I lost my nerve."

Twice that week McGee had planned to talk to her coach but had chickened out each time. On Monday she had had a bad day on the ice. She missed two easy shots on goal in scrimmage and Coach Briggs had given her a really scalding look. She decided not to say anything about the ballet then because he might accuse her of not concentrating enough on the game.

Then on Tuesday, their goalie, Jason Walcott, had fallen with his legs spread out in the splits trying to block a slap shot. Coach Briggs joking referred to him as "Twinkle Toes." That had clinched it. She wasn't about to let him call her that.

"But, McGee," Gwen wailed, "what about the Bunheads and our plan?"

"I'm sorry, Gwen." McGee's voice was hardly a whisper. "Tell the gang to go on without me."

"What am I supposed to do with your share of the pizza and snacks?" Gwen demanded, staring at the table full of food.

"Just eat 'em, I guess." A loud whistle sounded in the background and McGee said, "Got to run. See you."

The receiver clicked in her ear and Gwen listened to the dial tone. A horrible fear gripped her. What if everyone called and canceled? The very first party she had ever thrown would be a total disaster! Her mother would never get over it.

Luckily, the doorbell rang before she had time to talk herself into a total panic. Gwen covered the distance from the kitchen to the front door in record time.

"Greetings, salutations, and welcome!" Gwen sang out, imitating Mr. Lo as she flung the front door open.

Rocky, Zan and Mary Bubnik stood together on the front step. Behind them was Mary Bubnik's mother. "Come on downstairs," Gwen said. "The snacks should be ready any minute now."

Mrs. Hays appeared and, after being introduced

to everybody, invited Mary's mother into the living room for coffee. Rocky, Mary, and Zan helped Gwen carry the trays of food into the basement.

"Is your father in the Air Force?" Rocky asked once they reached the bottom of the stairs.

"No, why?"

"Your house would pass my dad's 'white glove' inspection."

Gwen laughed. "That's my mother. She's obsessed with cleanliness. But make yourself at home. She promised not to vacuum again until after the party."

"Where's McGee?" Zan asked, after surveying the large recreation room.

"Trapped," Gwen announced. She set a large bowl of pretzels on the table and scooped up a handful. "She's at hockey practice."

"With the Fairview Express?" Rocky raised her eyebrows.

Gwen nodded and passed around the plate full of cheese crackers. "The coach scheduled practice at the last minute."

"I don't understand," Mary Bubnik said, taking a small nibble out of her cracker. "Doesn't she realize how important this rehearsal is to us?"

"She does," Gwen said, grabbing another handful of pretzels. She shoved them in her mouth and mumbled, "But she's afraid."

Zan cocked her head. "Of what? That her coach will kick her off the team?"

"No." Gwen hesitated. "Well, yes and no. I think she's worried that he'll call her a wimp for being in *The Nutcracker*."

Rocky's dark eyes flashed. "I don't like people calling my friends sissies."

"No one's called her anything yet," Gwen cautioned. "She's just afraid the coach will if he finds out."

"So what are we going to do about the rehearsal?" Mary Bubnik asked as she dipped a chip into a bowl of ranch dressing. "I mean, McGee's the only one of us who really knows the steps."

Rocky took a swig of her Coke. "I say we go get her."

"What?" Mary choked on her chip. "Just march ourselves into that hockey rink and grab her?"

"Why not?" Rocky shrugged.

Gwen put her hands on her hips. "Well, in the first place, Coach Briggs won't allow it."

"Wait a minute!" Zan smiled mysteriously. "He will once he hears our tragic news."

"What news is that?" Mary Bubnik watched Zan slowly pace in a circle around the room. "Are you making this up? What news?"

Zan put one finger delicately to her lips and turned to face the group. "The news about McGee's

103

grandmother being terribly sick." She raised her eyebrows. "Near death, in fact."

Gwen's face lit up and she joined Zan in making believe. "Only one person can save her now!"

Zan nodded. "Her beloved granddaughter, McGee."

Rocky threw herself on the couch, with one hand over her heart. In her best little old lady voice, she croaked, "If I could only see my darling little McGee one more time..."

"Aw, that's so sad," Mary Bubnik said. "Just thinking about it makes me feel awful."

"Let's hope her coach feels that way and lets her out of practice," Zan said seriously.

"Wait a minute!" Rocky sat up with a start. "What if he asks who we are?"

Gwen snapped her fingers. "We'll say we're McGee's cousins."

"Uh-oh," Zan said. "What about me? I'm black."

"Distant cousins," Mary Bubnik drawled without missing a beat.

They all laughed.

"It's necessary that we be convincing," Zan added. "You know, some of us should be struggling to hold back tears."

"That's easy," Gwen said. "The hard part is cranking them out."

"Think of something sad," Rocky said, remembering the acting class she had taken out at the air base. "Like your dog dying."

"I don't have a dog," Gwen complained.

"Then think about your cat!"

Gwen squeezed her eyes tight for a full minute. Finally she opened them and said, "Sorry, I don't feel anything."

Rocky pinched her hard on the arm. "You feel that?"

"Ouch!" Gwen yelped. "That hurt!" Then she looked up and declared, "Hey, it worked. See?"

Mary and Zan leaned forward to look into her eyes. Behind her thick glasses, Gwen's brown eyes were definitely brimming with tears.

"Poking yourself in the eye also works," Rocky advised. "It's always good to throw in a few sniffs just to make it really convincing."

Just then, Mrs. Hays appeared at the basement door with a plate of cucumber sandwiches.

Thinking fast, Gwen turned to her mother and cried, "Mom, it's McGee. She called from the Fairview Ice Arena. She can't come to rehearsal unless someone gives her a ride." Gwen added a hiccup-like sob to the end of her sentence for greater effect.

"Well, that's certainly nothing to get upset about," Mrs. Hays said. When Gwen quivered her chin her mother added, "Why don't you girls grab your coats, and Mrs. Bubnik and I will drive you over there right away."

"Thanks, Mom." Gwen sniffed and wiped her nose on the sleeve of her blouse. "You're great."

The moment Mrs. Hays disappeared up the basement stairs. Gwen cried out with glee, "It worked!"

Minutes later the four girls were seated in the back of Mrs. Hays' white Cadillac. The ice arena was only a ten-minute drive away. As they sped along, the four girls whispered quietly in the backseat.

"Who should be the one to do all the talking?" Gwen asked.

"I don't think I could possibly do it," Zan said quickly.

"What do you mean?" Gwen protested. "It was your idea!"

"It may have been my idea, but you know McGee much better than we do, Gwen," Zan said. "I think you should be the one."

"Me?" Gwen squeaked. "Talk in front of a bunch of guys? I couldn't." She shook her head. "We need someone tough. Someone who won't back down from the challenge."

They all turned to face Rocky.

"OK," she sighed. "I'll do the talking. But you guys better back me up."

"You know you can count on us," Mary Bubnik promised.

Chapter Eleven

"Wait a minute, wait a minute," Gwen huffed just as Rocky reached the doors of the ice arena. "Let's go over our plan of action one more time."

"What's to go over?" Rocky asked. "We get in, get it over with, and get out. With McGee."

"Just remember," Mary Bubnik said, "we're right behind you."

Rocky swung open the glass door and the gang stepped inside. They stood in the lobby, trying to figure out how to get to the rink. There were several doors to choose from. Rocky shrugged and tried the one nearest her. It opened into a long dark tunnel. "This way," she ordered.

"Are you sure you know where we're going?"

Gwen asked, as they felt their way down the dimly lit corridor. Rocky gestured toward the end of the tunnel, where the sound of a whistle blowing and noisy shouting could be heard.

"This place is kind of scary," Zan muttered under her breath.

"Don't say things like that," Mary Bubnik cautioned. "My mother says I have a very vivid imagination."

Just then a door opened beside them and the hall was bathed in a bright white light. A frightening creature stood in the doorway. His legs and arms were huge and bulky, like they were deformed. Worst of all, he had no face but a white ghostly mask with little slits for eyes. Mary Bubnik took one look at the menacing stick in his hand and screamed.

"AAAAAAAAHHHHHHHH!"

She turned and raced for the end of the tunnel with Zan and Gwen hot on her heels. Mary burst through the door and flew headlong onto the ice, sliding right into the middle of a group of similarly dressed creatures.

"Don't hit me!" she bawled as they skated around her to see if she was all right. One of the bulky monsters knelt down beside her.

"Hey, Mary, it's OK," a familiar voice said. Peeking out from under the shiny plastic helmet were two brown braids.

"McGee!"

"Haven't you ever seen a hockey player before?" McGee asked, as she helped Mary Bubnik stand up.

Mary shook her head. "Only in those awful scary movies where guys with faces like that," she said, pointing to the goalie in his mask, "run around attacking kids on Halloween."

"What's going on here?" a deep male voice demanded. Mary Bubnik looked up to see a beefy man with a whistle around his neck, glaring at her.

"It's all right, Coach," McGee spoke up. "She's a friend of mine."

"I gathered that," he said. "What on earth is she doing out here disrupting team practice?"

"Oh, my goodness, I completely forgot!" Mary exclaimed. "We came to rescue McGee."

"We?" the man repeated.

Mary Bubnik gestured to Rocky, Zan, and Gwen who were gingerly making their way out onto the ice.

"And what do you mean, 'rescue McGee'?"

"You see, it's like this," Mary Bubnik said quickly. "A terrible thing has happened. Her grandmother is beside herself with death – "

A loud groan came from the three girls. Mary Bubnik looked over and caught Zan shaking her head. "*Near* death" she muttered, "not beside – "

"Whatever," Mary Bubnik went on. "Anyway, all I'm saying is, McGee has to go home right now."

"She does, huh?" The coach was starting to look very irritated. "What's all this about, McGee?"

"I don't know, Coach," McGee shrugged. Her ears were starting to burn with embarrassment. A few of her teammates were snickering and the rest had broad grins on their faces.

"Is this your idea of a joke?" Coach Briggs asked Mary Bubnik. "We've got important business here. This team has got to practice."

"So do we!" Rocky blurted out, then clapped her hand over her mouth.

"What do you mean?" he demanded. "I thought her grandmother was sick." He mimicked Mary Bubnik's voice. "Beside herself, in fact."

"Uh...uh..." Rocky looked desperately at Gwen and Zan, begging them to help her out.

"Th – that's why we have to practice," Gwen stammered. "For the funeral."

The whole team burst out laughing. The coach shut them up with a sharp look, then turned on Gwen. "I don't need any smart-aleck remarks from you, young lady." He glared at the rest of them. "Or some bogus story, either."

Jason Walcott slipped his goalie's mask off his head and said, "Funny friends you've got there, McGee."

"Yeah." McGee looked at them. Gwen was blinking nervously behind her thick glasses. Rocky had her hands stuck in her pockets and her hair was a wild tangled mass around her head. Zan was trying to hide behind the others. Mary Bubnik's lower lip started quivering and her eyes were close to tears. For a moment, McGee felt embarrassed to admit she knew them.

Then a funny feeling came over her. Rocky, Zan, Gwen and Mary Bubnik had gone to all of this trouble just for her. They had endured being humiliated in front of the team, and being yelled at by the coach, all for her sake. McGee couldn't think of anyone else who would have done the same.

She skated between Coach Briggs and the forlorn girls. "Coach, it's all my fault."

"Your fault?"

"They were just trying to help me out of a jam," she explained. "If you want to yell at someone, you can yell at me." McGee looked him straight in the eye. "Just don't yell at my friends."

He looked at her but didn't say anything.

"You see, we're in *The Nutcracker* at the dance academy – "

"I didn't know you were a ballet dancer," the coach interrupted. "That's – "

McGee cut him off before he could say anything more. "My mom made me do it, but anyway, I'm in it." She pointed to the gang. "We're all in it, together. That's why I had to miss practice before, because we had rehearsal. I didn't tell you or the team because I was afraid everybody'd think I was a sissy."

McGee looked at her teammates to see if anyone was laughing at her. No one said a word.

"Until a couple of weeks ago, hockey was the most important thing in my life." McGee glanced over at Gwen and continued. "Well, I'm realizing that my friends are just as important. And at this moment they need me more than the Express does. I can't let them down."

The coach nodded, but didn't say anything. He just kept staring at her.

"So I'm going to leave practice now 'cause we were supposed to rehearse our dance this afternoon." McGee swallowed hard and added, "If you want to kick me off the team, OK. But that's what I'm going to do."

McGee turned and started to skate off the ice when a booming voice stopped her.

"KATHRYN MCGEE!" Her name echoed around the ice arena. "Hold it right there. I didn't say you could leave."

McGee's knees locked and she grimaced, waiting for the worst.

"First of all," Coach Briggs said in a steady voice, "if you want something, you *ask* me. You don't *tell* me."

"Yes, sir." McGee dug at the ice with the blade of her skate. Her courage was dissolving fast.

"Is that absolutely clear?"

"Yes, Coach." McGee's voice was barely audible.

"Now, the next time you have ballet rehearsal, just ask me, OK? And, if I can, I'll excuse you from hockey practice."

"You will?" McGee couldn't believe her ears.

Coach Briggs nodded. "Dancing is good for your hockey. Reflexes, stamina, flexibility, the works." He looked around at his team. "Some of you jokers ought to try it. Especially you, Jason." Coach Briggs grinned at the goalie. "You need all the flexibility you can get."

He turned back to McGee and punched her lightly on her padded shoulder. "Now get out of here before I change my mind."

McGee led the gang to side of the rink. "Give me a second to change, OK?" She looked proudly at her friends. "Thanks for coming to get me."

Gwen cleared her throat. "What are friends for?"

Minutes later all five of them were crammed together in the backseat of the car. Everyone was talking at once, trying not to let the mothers in front hear any details.

"And then when I fell out onto the ice," Mary Bubnik giggled, "I thought we were going to get in trouble for sure."

"You don't call what happened back there trouble?" Rocky whispered. They all started giggling.

"Well, the important thing," Zan concluded, "is that we're back together."

"Yeah," McGee agreed, "and we still have time to practice the mouse dance."

"Right after we eat the pizza," Gwen reminded them. "Piping hot right out of the oven." Her eyes grew as wide as saucers. "Oven? Oh, NO!"

"I just can't believe both of those beautiful, deluxe pizzas were ruined!" Gwen put her head in her hands and moaned. They were back in the basement of the Hays' house. Most of the smoke had cleared out of the kitchen but there was still a smell of singed pepperoni in the air.

McGee, who was sitting beside her on the couch, patted Gwen on the back. "You're lucky you set the oven at two hundred instead of four hundred degrees."

"What's so lucky about it?" Gwen peeked out from behind her fingers. "They still got burned up."

"Well, the pizzas may be gone," Mary Bubnik explained, "but at least your house is still here. You should be thankful for that."

"Besides," Zan added, reaching for another cheese cracker, "you still have all this other delicious food."

114

"But the pizza was supposed to be the main course," Gwen pouted.

"Forget the pizza," Rocky called from the center of the room. "Who remembers which foot we start on in the dance?"

"I do," McGee replied. She jumped up to join Rocky. "The right one, of course."

"What? That's not it."

"No, no, I swear it's the right."

Rocky shook her head. "I think it's the left foot."

"Rocky." McGee crossed her arms. "All dances start on the right foot."

"Says who?" Rocky demanded.

"Says me," McGee shot back. "Everybody knows that."

"Oh, yeah? What if you're left-footed?" Rocky retorted.

"Well, let's take a vote," McGee compromised. "What do you say, Mary Bubnik?"

"You're asking *me*?" Mary recoiled in shock at the thought. "I don't know, I can't tell my right from my left." A worried frown creased her forehead. "It really is a problem for me, trying to remember."

"Maybe we can do something to help you," McGee said, tossing one of her braids over her shoulder. "You know, figure out some sort of turn signal."

"Like, just before we turn right," Rocky said, "we all raise our right paw." She demonstrated the maneuver.

"Great," Zan said, wiping the crumbs from her hands as she arose from the couch. "Let's try it."

Gwen joined them and they formed a single line down the center of the room. "Everybody ready?' McGee, who was in front, called out. "One, two, step, hop."

Just before their first turn, Rocky sang out, "Right paw!" and they all raised their right hand. "And turn!" Mary and the others followed McGee in a perfect turn. "It worked!" Mary Bubnik squealed. "Y'all don't realize what a help that is for me!"

They started the opening of their dance again when suddenly Rocky cried out, "Hold it!"

"What's the matter?" Gwen asked. "I thought we were doing great."

"Well, it's like this," Rocky said slowly. "You were just a teeny bit slow at the start. I almost ran into you."

Gwen blushed bright pink. "Well, I can't help it. I get behind because I'm so, uh...short, my legs don't move as fast as yours."

"Then why don't you start just a fraction ahead of the count," McGee suggested. "You know, give yourself a running start."

Gwen's face brightened. "I'll try it."

"While we've stopped," McGee added, "Zan,

you really should stand up straight when you take the lead."

The smile on Zan's face melted as she stared down at the ground. "I'm just so unbearably tall, I feel like I'm blocking everybody."

"Here, try staying just a little behind McGee," Rocky said, gently pushing Zan into position behind McGee. "That way it'll be the two of you going forward together." They tried two *jetés* and a run, run, leap.

"How'd that feel?" Rocky asked.

"Lots better," Zan admitted. "Thanks."

They ran through the dance several more times, making sure to give Gwen a head start, and use all the proper turn signals for Mary Bubnik. Zan improved noticeably once she thought the focus wasn't on her.

"That time was the best we've ever done it," McGee announced after they finished the last time.

"This is kind of fun, huh?" Gwen said. Her face was flushed with excitement. "For the first time I feel like I know what I'm doing."

"Me, too!" Mary Bubnik agreed. "And that's a miracle!"

Everyone laughed. Rocky clapped her hands together to get their attention. "Okay, we've got the moves, now we add the acting. Scrinch up your noses real hard and show your teeth, like rats do."

117

"Add a sound, too," Zan suggested. "That some-times helps."

"GRRRRR!" Gwen growled at Mary Bubnik, who burst out laughing.

"What's so funny?" Gwen shot Mary an indignant look. "That was supposed to scare you."

That made Mary Bubnik laugh so hard she could-n't stop. Then she got the hiccups and Rocky had to pound her on the back to get her to stop. She put her hand on her chest and gasped for breath. "Mercy! I guess you could say I was scared silly."

This sent Zan and McGee over the edge. They growled at each other in their best rat voices between fits of laughter. Within moments even Gwen had joined the fun.

"Girls, it's time to go home," Mrs. Bubnik called from the top of the basement steps. "Are you ready?"

"Ready as we'll ever be," McGee called out. She turned to face the gang. "Guess the party's over."

"This was really fun, Gwen," Zan said as they put on their coats.

"Thanks." Gwen felt really proud that her first party had been a success.

"The next time we'll see each other is Saturday," Mary Bubnik reminded everyone. "I get nervous chills just thinking about doing the mouse dance for Miss Jo and the Bunheads."

"I'm going to go home and practice every minute," Zan promised.

"Me, too," the rest chorused.

They stood together in a little circle at the foot of the basement steps for a moment. No one wanted to leave.

Finally Rocky thrust her hand out in the middle of the circle.

"One for all," she said solemnly, looking into each girl's face.

McGee put her hand on top of Rocky's first. Then came Mary Bubnik, Zan, and Gwen.

Together, they said, "And all for one."

Chapter Twelve

"Well done, girls," Miss Jo called out as McGee and the gang finished the last steps of the mouse dance. "Wonderful improvement!"

The five friends stood together by the *barre*, listening in delight to the applause from the other young dancers. Mrs. Bruce smiled at them from the piano. Even Alice Wescott started to applaud but stopped when Page Tuttle pinched her arm.

"At this rate, you should be absolutely perfect by Saturday's performance."

At the mention of "performance," a nervous whispering rippled around the studio. Miss Jo smiled and nodded.

"Yes, *performance*. Today is our final rehearsal

before the entire company moves into the auditorium. From now on, you will be dealing with costumes – "

She paused as another wave of giggling went around the room.

"Scenery, lights, and many more dancers. It will be confusing, difficult and very exciting!"

Miss Jo's voice took on a new seriousness. "For two performances you will become the official members of a professional ballet company. It is a big responsibility."

McGee swallowed hard. For the first time she sensed the importance of the whole event. One quick glance at the others showed they were feeling the same way.

"Now, today we have a special treat for you," Miss Jo announced. "The principal dancers have invited us to watch them rehearse several dances from the second act."

A changed group of girls followed Miss Jo to the other studio. As official company members, each girl held her chin high and pointed her toes.

The rehearsal was already in progress as the children tiptoed into the studio and sat down along the walls.

Derek McClellan lifted Clara from a beautiful painted sleigh. The music swelled from a speaker in the corner, filling the room with lilting sound.

"They must have just arrived in the Kingdom of

Sweets," Zan whispered to the others. "Now the Cavalier will take Clara to his castle."

Clara's face glowed with wonder as she rested her head on his shoulder. Gently he carried her in his arms toward the throne.

"He sure is handsome!" Mary Bubnik sighed. "I'd give anything to play the part of Clara."

Gwen and Zan nodded agreement. They held their breaths as Clara and the cavalier danced a *pas de deux* by the throne.

The music shifted from the romantic mood of the duet to a bright and lively rhythm. "Watch this," Zan whispered. "All of the dances are named after delicious things to eat. The Candy Canes are first."

Two dancers dressed in striped leotards and tights sprung onto the dance floor. They leaped in and out of the red-and-white hoops, rolling them across the floor and twirling them above their heads in clever ways.

"That was neat!" McGee clapped loudly as the dancers made their exit.

The music changed again, this time to a slow mysterious melody played by an oboe. Three girls slinked across the floor with chiffon scarves across their faces.

"They look like harem girls," Gwen whispered.

"They are," Zan replied. "This is the Arabian Coffee Dance."

The dancers wove their arms and bodies in and

out of each other in complicated patterns. It was like watching the flames in a fire.

"I think I'd like to do that dance," Mary Bubnik declared at the music's end.

"I thought you wanted to be Clara," Gwen said.

"Well, if I can't be Clara," Mary Bubnik said, "I'd like to be an Arabian Coffee dancer."

The Chinese dance was very funny. The dancers hopped around the room in shiny green silk pajamas with Chinese straw hats, pointing their fingers toward the ceiling.

"I wouldn't want to do that one," Gwen muttered to Rocky. "It looks too much like jogging."

Rocky's eyes were glued to three handsome guys waiting by the far wall. They were wearing high black boots and military coats with tall fur hats. She nudged Zan. "Who are those guys?"

"They're Cossacks," Zan whispered back. "Oooh, this must be the Russian Dance. It's my favorite."

The trio of dancers exploded into the room with the first chord of music. Keeping their arms crossed, they squatted down front and kicked their legs out in from of them. Each got a solo. One spun in a circle, hopping on one leg with the other extended out to the side. His partner leaped into the air with his legs outstretched and touched his toes. The last one did back handsprings diagonally across the studio and ended with a back flip.

"That was fantastic!" McGee squealed. "Kind of like break-dancing and gymnastics rolled into one."

"Mr. Lo was right," Gwen added. "Ballet is for athletes!"

The delicate music of the Sugar Plum Fairy tinkled in the air. The girls held their breaths as she danced, lighter than air, darting from one *piqué* turn to another. She fluttered gracefully into her final pose.

"Oh, how wonderful!" Zan breathed. "She looks like an angel."

Now it was time for the Sugar Plum Fairy and the Cavalier to dance together. "Do you think they're in love?" Mary Bubnik wondered out loud.

"Most definitely," Zan replied. "Look at the way he watches her every move."

The Sugar Plum Fairy *bourréed* forward in little tiny steps. The Cavalier was right behind her, his hands resting gently on her waist. Then she unfolded her arms and twirled in a beautiful pirouette.

"One, two, three – *four* turns," Rocky counted in awe.

When the ballerina ran lightly toward the Cavalier and leaped into the air, they all gasped. He lifted her above his head and carried her in a slow circle around the room.

"Either he's really strong," Gwen marveled, "or she doesn't weigh a thing. I wonder what she eats?"

"Most dancers are always on diets," Zan said.

"You're kidding!" McGee exclaimed. "They look like skinny birds."

"They get weighed every time they rehearse." Zan pointed to a scale standing by the window at the far end of the studio.

"That is the most gruesome thing I have ever heard," Gwen hissed.

"Well, it's true."

Gwen's eyes widened. "You mean, they even weigh guest company members like us?" Her mind raced ahead to possible excuses to avoid being weighed, like calling in sick or pretending to faint as she approached the scale.

Zan laughed. "They only weigh the professionals."

Then it was time for the Waltz of the Flowers. The music began and, one by one, the older dancers floated across the room in waltz time. Courtney and the Bunheads waited their turn by the window, looking very nervous.

"I hope they do OK," Mary Bubnik whispered, half to herself and half out loud.

Zan nodded agreement. Rocky and McGee exchanged funny looks. They were all having the same feeling. Now that they were full-fledged members of the ballet, it was very important that everything go right in *The Nutcracker*.

Courtney and Page began their circle, waltzing around the room. They did a whole series of *chainé* turns, spinning in a diagonal across the floor. After they had finished, Rocky and McGee led the gang in a round of applause.

Courtney shot them a suspicious look. When she realized they weren't making fun, her face broke into a very surprised smile.

The second act came to a close and they all cheered. The lead dancers playfully took a bow and the gang applauded extra loud for the Sugar Plum Fairy. Then Miss Jo announced that rehearsal was over.

"Remember, next Saturday morning will be our dress rehearsal," Miss Jo told them. "It's the only time that we could reserve Patterson Auditorium and the orchestra. Then we open that afternoon! So go home and gets lots of rest."

"Oh, I can't bear to go home right away," Zan exclaimed. They had changed into their street clothes and were standing on the sidewalk in front of Hillberry Hall.

"Me, neither," Mary Bubnik said. "I feel like dancing forever!" Shutting her eyes, she waltzed in a tiny circle on the sidewalk.

"Watch where you're going," a voice cried out.

Mary Bubnik opened her eyes too late and collided into Courtney Clay. Page Tuttle and the rest of the Bunheads were standing behind her.

"Oh, look what you've done!" Courtney complained. "Now you've messed up my hair." A single stray loop hung down from the back of her tightly rolled bun.

"Oh, I'm sorry," Mary apologized. "Gosh, your Waltz of the Flowers dance was just beautiful. I was so impressed."

Courtney smiled and said simply, "Dancing is my life."

Gwen buried her head in Rocky's hair and murmured softly in her ear, "I think I'm going to gag."

McGee stepped forward. "Courtney, I think we should call a truce."

"Do you really?" She arched her eyebrow. "How nice."

"No, really," Zan chimed in. "We all want the same thing – a truly wonderful production of *The Nutcracker.*"

"Right now we're even," Rocky said. "You guys got us once and we got you."

"Let's just leave it like that," McGee finished. "What do you say?"

"Maybe you're right," Courtney said. "Playing pranks is so juvenile, anyway."

"That's a relief," Mary Bubnik said. "Now we can all be friends."

Courtney asked, "Have you guys seen your costumes yet?"

"No," Zan said. "Are they ready?"

"Yes," Page Tuttle replied. "And they are – "

"Unbelievable," Courtney finished for her.

"Really?" Mary Bubnik exclaimed.

The Bunheads nodded emphatically.

"What do they look like?" Rocky asked.

"Did you ever see the musical, *Cats*?" Courtney asked.

"Yes, it was fabulous," Zan cried. "You mean, our mouse costumes are like that?"

Courtney smiled. "They're even better."

Rocky cocked her head. "What do cats have to do with our mouse suits?"

"Oh, everything!" Zan exulted. "In the musical, all of the dancers wear sleek, shiny leotards."

McGee perked up, "Really?"

Zan nodded. "Yes, with wild colorful shoes and wigs – "

"And fantastic makeup," Page added.

"I like that," Gwen giggled.

"I'd really like a tail that I could snap like a whip," Rocky said. "Do you think we'll have tails?"

Courtney nodded. "I'm sure you will."

Mary Bubnik hugged her dance bag to her chest. "Oh, I wish we could see them right now!"

"You'll just have to wait till next week," Page said.

"Yes," Courtney agreed. "That way it will be a surprise."

The gang waved merrily as Courtney and her friends skipped off down the street.

"Boy, I can't tell you how glad I am that we're not

fighting with those Bunheads anymore," Mary Bubnik sighed.

Gwen nodded. "Now we can concentrate on our performance."

"And the best part is yet to come," Mary Bubnik gushed. "Next Saturday we'll be wearing *real* costumes."

"On a *real* stage," Rocky joined in.

"In a *real* theatre," McGee added.

"Dancing our hearts out to a *real* live orchestra," Zan gushed.

"In front of *real* people!" Gwen finished.

They all gasped as one. "People?"

"Oh, no," Mary Bubnik groaned. "One more thing to worry about."

"What's that?" Gwen asked.

"Stage fright!"

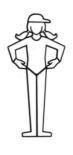

"Stand up, please!" Mrs. Phelps, the wardrobe mistress, ordered. She was in charge of all the costumes for the ballet. "Now, face me!"

Five miserable girls stood in a row before her in the costume shop of the civic auditorium.

"I can't believe we fell for the Bunheads' trick," Rocky said, staring at her costume in the mirror. "These are ugly with a capital 'Ugh.'"

"How could they put me in a fat suit?" Gwen was near tears as she pointed to the padded belly in her mouse costume. It looked like a large innertube had been wrapped around her entire middle.

"What you care to trade?" Zan's sleeves were too

short and the old flannel costume sagged everywhere on her lanky body.

"This will never do." Mrs. Phelps grabbed a handful of Zan's costume and shook it. "Could you gain ten pounds by this afternoon?"

Zan shrugged and stared down at her gray ballet slippers.

"Nobody told me we had to wear these ears!" McGee tugged at the hood that snapped under her chin. "I can't hear a thing!"

"I don't know. I think we look kind of cute." Mary Bubnik held her hands in front of her like paws and did a couple of practice hops.

"Cute?" Rocky shouted. "I think we look absolutely stupid!"

Courtney Clay stuck her head into their dressing room and giggled. "Oooh, look at the funny, fat rats!"

Three other heads peeked around the door. Each wore a little crown of flowers.

"Gosh," Mary Bubnik gushed, "y'all look beautiful!"

Courtney skipped into the room and twirled before them. Her pink chiffon skirt spun out in a perfect circle around her.

"Show off!" Rocky grumbled.

"You'll have to go back to your dressing room, girls!" Mrs. Phelps was on her knees, trying to pin Zan's costume. "It's too crowded in here."

"That's OK, Mrs. Phelps. We have to do our warm-up exercises." Courtney smiled sweetly at Rocky. "Some of us have to *dance* today."

"Some of us have to throw up!" Rocky stuck out her tongue as Courtney danced out of the room.

"Their costumes look brand-new!" Gwen pouted.

"They are." Mrs. Phelps peered over her bifocals. "These mouse costumes are all that remain from the original production ten years ago."

"Lucky us!" Rocky muttered under her breath.

"Speak up!" McGee leaned forward and squinted. "I still can't hear a thing."

"Here, try this." Rocky grabbed McGee's hood and yanked it back behind her ears. "Is that better?"

"Yes, but now I'm bald! You pulled my braid right out of my head."

A voice boomed over the loudspeaker, "Onstage for Act One!"

"Oh, dear," Mrs. Phelps said, sticking a few more pins in Zan's costume. "There's never enough time."

She tugged at McGee's sleeve, tried to straighten the padding on Gwen's costume, and then stepped back and surveyed the group. "After your rehearsal, go to your dressing rooms, and I'll stop in to fix your costumes."

"Can you fix them to like that?" Gwen pointed to a group of dancers passing the costume shop door. They were dressed in beautiful velvet dresses with little white pantaloons that peeked out beneath the hems.

"I recognize them," Rocky said. "They were at the audition."

Zan nodded sadly. "They were chosen to play the party guests."

Mary Bubnik sighed. "And we weren't."

The orchestra played the opening strains of *The Nutcracker*, and Mrs. Phelps shooed them toward the door. "Hurry up, you don't want to miss your entrance."

"Where do we go?" McGee asked, peering out into a long hallway.

"Down the hall, up those stairs and turn right. A chaperone will take you to the stage."

McGee led the mice down the hall past rows of dressing rooms. Each one had a sign-in sheet and pencil posted on the door.

"Oh, look!" Mary Bubnik pointed to the door nearest the stairs. "It says, Derek McClellan. Do you think he's in there?"

"Let's peek," Zan whispered. The two tiptoed toward the door.

"Wait a minute," Rocky said, grabbing a hold of Mary Bubnik's gray flannel tail. "Do you really want that handsome guy to see you dressed like a rat?"

Mary Bubnik looked down at her costume and squealed. "I forgot."

A pleasant, round-faced woman met them at the top of the stairs. She wore a name tag that read, Hello, I'm Blanche Maddox. Shining her flashlight on her clipboard, she said, "Let's see, you must be the mice."

"What was your first clue, Sherlock?" Gwen grumbled. She was still upset at being stuck in a fat suit and felt like taking it out on the world.

Mrs. Maddox shone her flashlight on the floor and led them through the darkness of backstage. They wound their way through the maze of dusty scenery and wooden boxes filled with lights and coiled wires. A balding man wearing a headset was sitting on a stool by a big metal control panel. Red and white lights blinked above rows of switches used to adjust the lights on the stage.

"Here are the mice," Mrs. Maddox whispered to the stage manager. He nodded and then pointed to a place in between two curtains.

"Have them wait in the wings," he said. "They're next." McGee stepped between the long black drapes. Her mouth dropped open as she saw the brightly lit stage in front of her. It was decorated to look like a Victorian house with a huge Christmas tree in back. Across the stage some men were busy pulling on thick ropes which caused the tree to grow larger and larger with each tug.

McGee was so enthralled that she didn't recognize their music being played by the orchestra. It sounded much different than Mrs. Bruce's piano version of a clock striking twelve.

"Go!" Gwen shrieked and shoved McGee in the back.

McGee stumbled forward onto the stage and was blinded by the light. The stage was huge, much bigger than their rehearsal studio. Her mind went blank and she froze in the center of the stage.

"Move!" Rocky ordered from behind her. McGee automatically started skipping. Zan was right on her heels trying to follow.

"Who's on my tail?" Gwen called. There was a tearing sound as she tugged it out from under Mary Bubnik's foot.

"Hold, please!" a voice shouted from the darkness of the auditorium. The orchestra stopped but the girls kept moving. "I said, *Stop!*"

All of the mice froze as Mr. Anton appeared at the edge of the stage.

"Where is your concentration?" he demanded in a tense voice. "I know it is difficult adjusting to the stage. But is this what you plan to do this afternoon? Do you realize we have an audience in exactly two hours?"

Luckily for the gang, he was distracted by a piece of scenery starting to topple. "Watch that wall!" Mr. Anton hopped up onto the stage to stop it from falling on Clara and the Mouse King. A stagehand

135

ran out from the wings, and Mr. Anton spoke with him for a few moments.

"If you hadn't shoved me, I would have been fine," McGee snapped at Gwen.

"Are you kidding? You were already late."

Mary Bubnik was near tears. "Nobody signaled. I just didn't know which way to go."

"I cannot believe I'm in a faded old rat costume about to perform before thousands of people," Zan moaned out loud.

"Me, neither," Gwen grumbled agreement. Then she turned to Rocky. "It's all your fault."

"My fault?" Rocky repeated.

"Yes, if you hadn't started that fight at the audition, we wouldn't be in this predicament."

Rocky lunged for Gwen, when Mary Bubnik jumped between them. "Please, I hate this! We shouldn't fight. We're friends, remember?"

"Silence!" Mr. Anton clapped his hands together and they snapped to attention. "Now we will do the dance again, yes?" He stared at them sternly. "And this time we will *concentrate!*"

They raced back into the wings, Mary Bubnik's last words ringing in their ears. No one spoke a word but, when the music began, McGee stepped out on time and she made sure she left room for Zan. Rocky gave Gwen a head start and they all remembered to signal for Mary Bubnik. When they exited, Courtney was waiting in the wings.

"Guess you mice need a little more practice," she said sweetly. "Well, you've still got an hour left before the audience arrives." She covered her smile with her hand.

Rocky stepped forward. "Yeah, and a lot can happen in an hour."

The pretty ballerina stopped smiling.

"Have you checked the resin box?" McGee asked innocently.

Courtney turned ash-white. She spun around and raced for her dressing room. Four Bunheads scurried right behind her.

"Well," Gwen cracked, "I feel better already."

Mrs. Maddox escorted them back to the stairs leading to their dressing room. "Now, you girls go take a break. I'll be back for you when the show starts."

Mary Bubnik threw open their dressing room door and squealed with delight. "Flowers! Someone sent us flowers, just like real ballerinas."

Five girls in heavily padded mouse costumes tried to squeeze through the door at once.

Each one of them had received a bouquet from her family.

Zan tore open the big box from her parents. A dozen roses rested on a bed of filmy paper.

"They're beautiful," Zan said, breathing in the sweet aroma as she hugged the wrapped flowers to her carefully.

137

"Mom remembered I love daisies! Aren't they pretty?" Mary Bubnik held up the yellow flowers arranged in a bright red basket. "Aren't they prettiest flowers you ever saw?"

"Of course you'd love daisies," Gwen said, "'cause you're so sunny all the time."

Mrs. Hays and Mrs. McGee had chosen identical arrangements of lovely red and green carnations for their daughters.

"Geez Louise," McGee giggled, "it looks like Christmas in here."

Gwen's mother had thrown in a plate of chocolate chip cookies with red and green M&Ms on top. "We all better have one right now," Gwen declared, opening the tin and passing it around. "For energy."

Rocky held up her family's gift, a ceramic pot wrapped in a big bow. Inside was a bright green cactus with a soft red blossom growing on top.

"What a perfectly perfect gift," Zan said, peering at it over Rocky's shoulder. "It's just like you."

"It is?"

Zan nodded. "A little prickly on the outside but a beautiful flower at heart."

Rocky turned her back and dabbed her eyes roughly. All five of them stood in silence, cradling their gifts. No one wanted to say a word.

Mary Bubnik was the first to notice the sixth arrangement resting on the makeup table.

"You guys, I think we missed one." She pointed to the poinsettia plant with a big green ribbon wrapped around its base. There was an envelope stuck into the foliage. McGee tore it open and read the card.

"Oh, no!" she groaned.

"What's it say?" Gwen asked.

"Break a leg," McGee replied in a dull voice.

"What?" Rocky shouted. "What kind of joke is that?"

"It's an old theatre tradition to keep away bad luck," Zan explained. "It really means good luck."

"Oh, yeah, right," Rocky mumbled. "I knew that. I just thought the Bunheads were trying to shake us up."

"Who is it from?" Gwen asked. "Your sisters?"

"Worse," McGee moaned. "The Express."

"Your team sent you a plant?" Mary Bubnik said. "Aw, that's sweet."

"It's from the coach." McGee handed the card to Rocky and slumped against the wall onto the linoleum floor.

Rocky read the card out loud. "We'll be in the audience today, cheering for the star – " She stopped and turned to McGee. "The star?"

McGee shrugged. "Well . . . yes."

Gwen arched her eyebrow. "The star?"

McGee looked up at her friends. "You see, after that big scene we made at the ice arena, the team has been razzing me for a week." She looked away and mumbled, "So I told them a teeny white lie."

"What did she say?" Mary Bubnik asked, tugging at her hood. "I couldn't hear that."

"She said she told them a *big fat lie*," Rocky sang out loud and clear.

"Oh?" Mary looked at McGee. "What lie was that?"

McGee covered her face with her hands. "That I was playing Clara."

"What?" they all shouted.

"How could you!" Zan demanded.

"I never in a trillion years thought they'd actually come!" McGee lay back on the floor and groaned. "I'll never, *ever* live this down!"

"I've got it," Zan said. "Call them right now and tell them the show's been canceled."

"Half hour to places!" a voice boomed out of the loudspeaker.

"Too late," Gwen said. "They're probably already in the auditorium."

Mrs. Phelps, the wardrobe mistress, tapped on the door and peered inside. She looked frazzled. "Any problems with your costumes?" She didn't wait for an answer. "Good. Now, here's your makeup." She placed a large red fishing tackle box on the edge of the dressing table.

"Makeup?" McGee's lip began to quiver. "I wish we were wearing masks!" She turned her back to the wall so no one could see her.

140

"I don't know how to do makeup." Mary Bubnik twirled her mouse tail anxiously.

"It's very simple," Mrs. Phelps explained, "Just put on a little mascara, some rouge, and pink lipstick."

Music began to play from the speaker above the door.

"That's the overture." Mrs. Phelps checked her wristwatch and stepped back into the hall. "Now, girls, don't miss your entrance."

"We won't!" they chorused.

Rocky flipped open the red metal box and they clustered around to peek inside,

Little tins and colored pencils sat in tiny compartments along the lid. On the bottom lay sponges and powder puffs.

"I think she made a mistake." Mary Bubnik held up a tube marked Grease Paint. "This looks like a painter's box."

"Grease paint is for the face," Zan explained in her soft voice. "A lot of actors and dancers use it."

"You mean, they paint on a whole new face?" Mary Bubnik's big blue eyes widened.

Zan nodded.

"Gosh, with all this stuff, we could really disguise ourselves!" McGee felt better already.

Gwen clapped her hands. "No one would ever know it was us!"

141

Rocky picked up a brown pencil and started drawing thick lines on her cheeks.

"What are you doing?" Mary Bubnik gasped.

"Drawing whiskers. If we're going to play rats, we might as well look like them."

Gwen and Mary Bubnik grabbed pencils and drew on big whiskers, too.

"What's this stuff?" McGee held up a black crayon and read the wrapper. "Tooth Black."

"Maybe you're supposed to put it on your teeth," Gwen advised.

McGee faced the mirror and very carefully colored in her front tooth. "Hey!" she giggled. "It looks like I was hit by a hockey puck."

"Let me try it!" Mary Bubnik reached for the crayon and blacked out all of her upper teeth.

"Ooh, that will really scare the little kids!" Gwen found more colored pencils and a compact mirror.

"The eyes are very important." Zan showed the others how to make pointed eyebrows with a pencil. The she took one of the tubes of yellow paint and covered her eyelids with it.

"That looks great!" Rocky snatched the blue tube and McGee grabbed the green one.

"Now we powder," Gwen instructed. "That's what Mom always does."

They passed the pink puff around the circle and big gusts of powder exploded into air.

"This is fun!" McGee and the others turned to smile at themselves in the mirror. Five ghoulish faces grinned back.

"It's absolutely perfect!" Gwen giggled.

"There's only one thing missing," Rocky said, cocking her head to look at everyone. "Dirt. We look too clean."

"Rocky's right," McGee agreed. "If we're going to look really ratty we should smear some dirt on our costume and rub our hands in it."

Gwen checked her watch. "We've still got a few minutes. Let's get some from the parking lot."

"The best way out is to the left," Zan said.

"How do you know that?" Rocky demanded. "Have you been here before?"

"No, but I read the fire escape instructions on the back of our door." Zan led them down the hall and up a different flight of stairs. "There should be an exit right" – she turned down another corridor – "here!"

In front of them stood a big door with a metal push handle. They swung it open and daylight streamed in on them. McGee picked up a brick lying just inside the door and handed it to Rocky. "Here, prop it open with this."

The girls tiptoed outside. They were standing by a platform marked Loading Dock. Behind them, the familiar music of the ballet carried from the stage through the door.

"This must be where they bring the scenery in," Rocky said, bending down to rub her hands in dirt.

"Wow!" McGee faced the parking lot. "Look at all those cars. The theatre must be packed!"

Zan quickly smeared dirt on her costume and said, "Come on, you guys. Let's get back. It's getting awfully close to our entrance."

Mary Bubnik clutched Zan's arm and whispered, "Do you notice something strange?"

"What?" Gwen asked, smudging her face with dirt.

"I don't hear any music."

Nobody moved. There was a deathly silence. Five girls in dusty padded mouse suits and gruesome makeup slowly turned to face the door. The brick was gone and the door shut tight.

"We're locked out!"

Chapter Fourteen

"It's no use," McGee said, after pummeling the door with her fists. "They can't hear us."

Mary Bubnik was frantic. "This is it. My dancing days are over before they've even begun." Her voice quivered. "My mother will send me back to Oklahoma. I'll never see any of you ever again."

"Don't say that!" McGee shouted at her. "We'll think of something."

"You'd better think fast," Zan said, glancing at her wristwatch. "According to my calculations – we're on!"

"Oh, great!" Gwen threw up her arms in the air. "This is just great!"

Rocky charged the door with a fierce karate kick. "Aieeyah!" Her foot bounced harmlessly off the thick metal.

"Give it up," McGee told her. "It's no use."

"Mrs. Maddox is probably running all over, looking for us," Mary Bubnik fretted. "But she's in the wrong place."

"We're going to have to find another way inside," Rocky declared.

"Well, the only other way I know to get in," Zan said, scratching her head, "is though the front door."

"Zan, you're a genius!" McGee started running down the alley toward the front of the building. "Follow me!"

"Hey, wait for me!" Gwen struggled to keep up with the others. She had enough trouble running in regular clothes, but in the padded mouse suit it was next to impossible.

McGee took the stairs two at a time and was the first one into the lobby of the theatre. She brushed past the usher in his blue uniform, shouting, "Out of our way! We're in the show!"

An elderly lady stormed out of the box office, fussing, "Just a minute! No one told me about this."

She narrowly escaped being mowed down by five determined mice. McGee threw open the main auditorium door, just as the clock chimes struck twelve. "This is it!"

As McGee ran down the aisle to the stage, a

woman turned and shrieked. McGee hesitated, then raised her arms above her head, and bared her blacked-out teeth.

Rocky, who was right behind her, turned to another spectator and did the same. Gwen, Mary Bubnik, and Zan joined them and soon the entire audience was shrieking and laughing in delight.

On stage, the Nutcracker and the dancers playing the toy soldiers didn't know what to do. At first they squinted out into the darkness of the auditorium, then quickly got into the spirit of the moment. The soldiers danced to the edge of the stage and pointed their bayonets at the audience who cheered.

The conductor in the orchestra pit spun in all directions, trying to see what was happening behind him. He spotted the girls and gestured for them to go to the stage immediately.

The gang was having too much fun to be scared. They danced merrily up the steps and arrived just in time for the part where they were chased in a circle by the toy soldiers.

McGee led them through each section with complete confidence, and they did every step perfectly. Rocky had never kicked so high. Gwen didn't fall behind once. Mary Bubnik didn't miss a turn. Zan threw her shoulders back and danced with all her might.

When Clara threw her shoe at the Mouse King, they were supposed to scurry off the stage. Rocky decided that would be a good time to try out her acting skills. She staggered to the wings, clutched the curtain and slid down it, mouthing, "They got me!"

The audience roared its approval. McGee and Gwen ran back onstage to die with her. They clutched their stomachs and fell forward onto Rocky. Then Zan and Mary Bubnik grabbed them by the feet and dragged them off the stage.

The auditorium rang with applause.

"Do you hear that?" Mary Bubnik cried, jumping up and down. "That's for us!"

"We did it!" Gwen squealed.

"I can't believe I just danced in front of thousands of people and wasn't nervous once!" Zan fell against the backstage wall in amazement.

Mary Bubnik suddenly put her hand over her mouth. "Boy, are we going to get in trouble with Mr. Anton."

"Not when we tell him we were locked out," Gwen replied.

"He'll understand." McGee gestured toward the auditorium. "I mean, listen to that applause."

Off in the darkness, there was a sudden rustle of movement. The girls glimpsed a bit of pink chiffon disappear behind the drape.

"You see that?" Rocky pointed to the spot where Courtney had been standing.

"Do you think she took the brick out of the door?" Mary Bubnik whispered.

"We'll never know for sure," Zan said. "But if she did, it certainly backfired on her!"

"Because we're a hit," Gwen whispered. The five mice wrapped their arms around each other and hopped soundlessly in a jubilant circle.

After the performance was over their dressing room was swamped with well-wishers. The first visitors were Coach Briggs and the entire Fairview Express hockey team.

"Nice going, McGee!" Jason the goalie said, punching her on the shoulder. "That was really cool, the way you came down the aisle and scared all those little kids."

"Thanks." McGee thought she would burst with happiness.

"Hey, do you think they'd let guys do those parts?" Casey Caldwell, one of the best-looking guys on her team, asked.

"I don't know," McGee replied. "You'd have to try out for it next year." She smiled and added, "If you're good enough, you might get cast."

"Well, I wouldn't want to play anything but the rats," Jason declared. "They were really gory."

"Especially the death scene," Casey added. "That was the best!"

"That was Rocky's idea." McGee looped her arm over her friend's shoulder. Rocky looked down at the floor and murmured shyly. "It was nothing, really."

After the team cleared out they heard a gentle voice in the hall. "Excuse me, could you direct me to the dressing room of the stars of the show?"

The girls recognized the voice and sang out at the top of their lungs, "Hi, Hi!"

The little Chinese man stuck his head around the door. "Salutations and greetings!" He was grinning from ear to ear. "Let me be the first to congratulate you on your great success. As they say in China, you really knocked 'em dead!"

The girls giggled and Zan said, "We owe a lot to you, Hi."

"You're a real pal," Rocky said, punching him lightly on the shoulder.

Mr. Lo blushed a deep red. "It would be a great honor if you and your families would come to my place for a celebration dinner."

"What's today's special?" Gwen asked.

"For you?" He grinned. "Hi Lo's Chinese pizza with *six* secret ingredients."

"We'll be there!" Gwen squealed. "After that exhausting performance, I'm starved!"

After he'd left, Mary Bubnik turned to the group with tears in her eyes. "I'm going to miss y'all so much."

"Why?" McGee asked. "You're not really moving back to Oklahoma, are you?"

Mary Bubnik shook her curly, blond head. "No, but we have one more performance tomorrow night and then that's it."

"That's not *it*." Rocky said fiercely. "We've got each other's numbers. We'll call and get together."

"But it won't be the same." Mary's lips quivered.

"That's true," Gwen said. "We won't see Miss Jo, or Hi Lo – "

"Or the Bunheads," McGee added.

Rocky stood up. "That settles it. We have to stay on at the Deerfield Academy."

"What do you mean?" Mary Bubnik asked.

"If we drop out now, the Bunheads will say we're quitters."

"That's true," Zan said.

McGee nodded. "They'll say we couldn't make the grade."

"Just think," Gwen said, "if we hadn't found each other, we probably *would* have dropped out of the ballet."

"And the audience would have missed our spectacular performance," Zan said.

"And the Bunheads would've won." Rocky hit her fist in her hand. "We've got to stay."

"Right!" McGee nodded.

Gwen raised one finger. "As I see it, there's only one, teensy problem."

"What's that?" They turned to face her.

"Our mothers," Gwen said. "How are we going to convince them to let us take classes here?"

McGee nodded. "That's right. They had to drag us here in the first place. They'll think something's fishy."

Zan put her hands on her hips. "We will just have to convince them that we've had a change of heart."

"That'll take some real acting," Rocky said.

Familiar voices and laughter echoed outside the dressing room.

"Oh, no!" Gwen whispered. "Our families. They're here!"

McGee and Rocky leaned against the door to hold it shut.

"Quick, think of something to tell them," Zan whispered.

Gwen groaned. "My mind's gone blank."

"I can't hold it much longer," Rocky warned.

Loud voices called, "Girls, let us in. What are you doing in there?"

McGee snapped her fingers. "I've got it!"

"Here they come!" Rocky fell back as the door swung open and their families burst into the room.

The four girls turned to McGee whose face was frozen in a smile. She spun to greet their parents and, with open arms, shouted, "We love ballet!"

About the Authors

JAHNNA N. MALCOLM stands for Jahnna "and" Malcolm. Jahnna Beecham and Malcolm Hillgartner are married and have published over 80 books for kids and teens. They've written about ballerinas, horses, ghosts, singing cowboys, and green slime. Their most recent book series is called *The Jewel Kingdom,* and it is about adventurous princesses. They even made a movie of the first book in that series, *The Ruby Princess Runs Away.*

Before Jahnna and Malcolm wrote books, they were actors. They met on the stage and were married on the stage, and now live in Oregon. They used to think of their ideas for their books by themselves. Now they get help from their son, Dash, and daughter, Skye.

You can write Jahnna and Malcolm on their website: www.jewelkingdom.com. They'd love to hear from you.

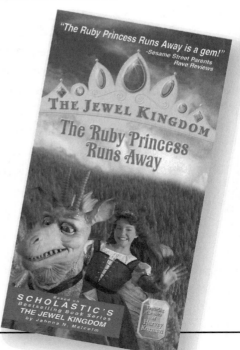